The Ballad of Omega Brown

by

Tom Vaine

The Ballad of Omega Brown

Copyright © 2025 by Tom Vaine

First Printing: November 2025

Published by **DarkWinter Press**: www.darkwinterlit.com

ISBN: 978-1-998441-35-8

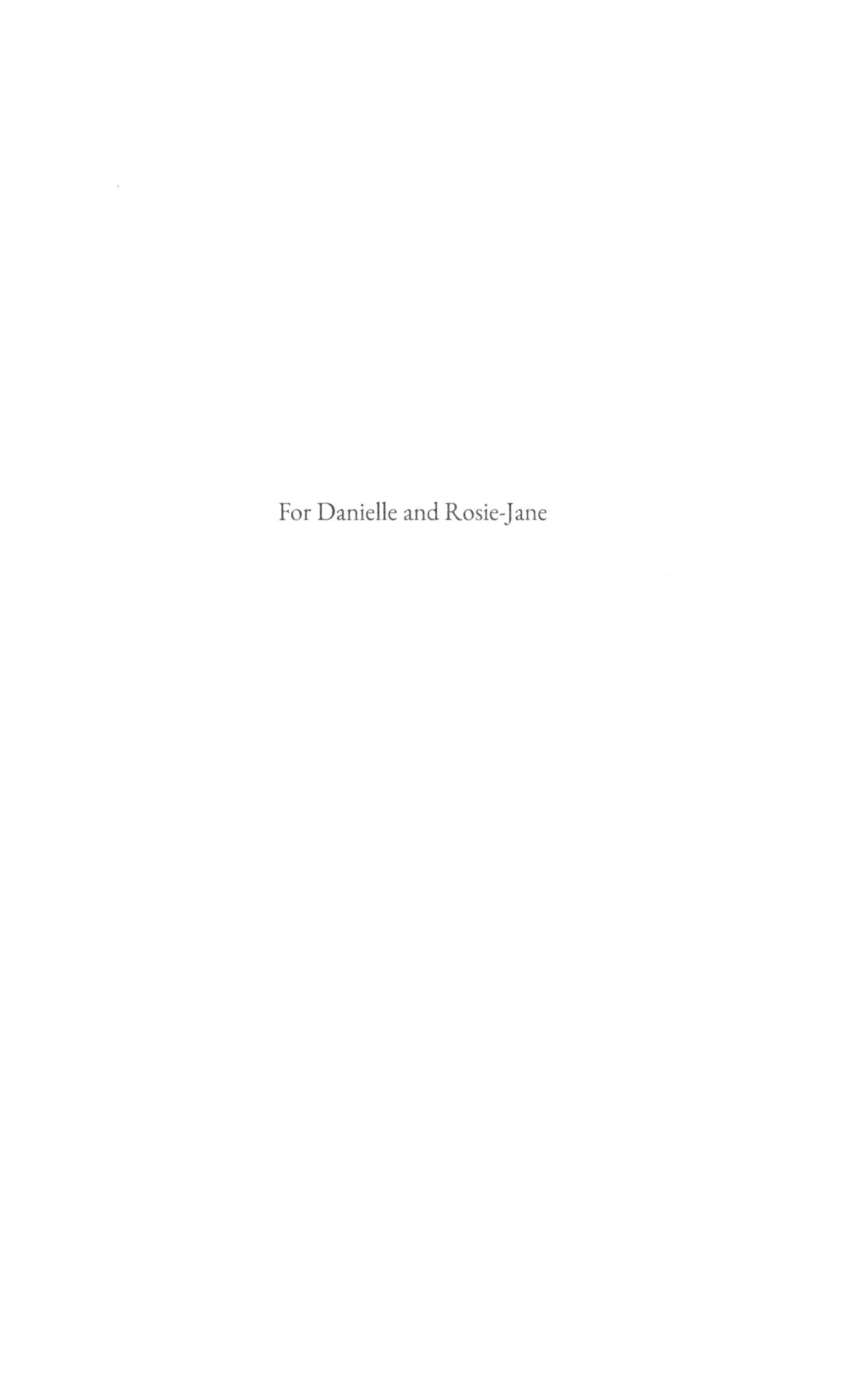

For Danielle and Rosie-Jane

Table of Contents

Episode 1:

The Lizardmen of Karackas

The sun was sinking low over the jungle horizon when Omega turned his pterosaur back towards the camp. Above him, the moons of Krildar VII seemed nearly as big as the planet itself; one of them even sharing its atmosphere. Omega squinted against the fading light to search the darkness around the moon called Karackas. It had been several cycles since the raiders' last incursion, but he had been told that they were hiding somewhere on or near that moon. The governing Corporation of this sector was sure of it.

Peering down, Omega saw that the jungle had grown totally dark. He shuddered at the thought of being alone among the trees now. The clinging heat and rough terrain, the constant insectoid humming that stopped only just before some awful monster struck. Not a pleasant place to be.

He had begun listing to himself the many ways in which bowels could be torn out when a laser bolt drove right into his lizard's head. The saurian gave one terrific honk before plummeting. The night sky was suddenly full of laser blasts and Omega, between bouts of g-force induced nausea, was a little baffled that his pursuers couldn't already tell how deep his predicament had become.

The first things to go would be the saddle buckles. The left side was easy enough but, by the time he got to the right, his mount had fallen into a worsening spin. The trees were doing somersaults now, and Omega could feel his eyes trying to find shelter in the back of his skull.

He relaxed into that spin and, as he felt the pressure of the remaining buckle loosen, pushed his feet against the lizard's back. The buckle slipped off and Omega watched his pterosaur's corpse begin free-falling away from him.

The shooting had stopped, but Omega was annoyed to find that he couldn't see its source. He was in the habit of keeping tabs on the people who shot at him. Instead, he focused on the quickly approaching forest. Surely, it would have better aim than his attackers.

Omega pulled his limbs in, making himself into a man-shaped bullet. He was hurtling downwards now, and the rush of the wind in his ears was so loud that he didn't notice he wasn't flying solo until the other was almost on top of him. A huge shadow, propelled by great hairy wings, shot down past him. The wind slapped at his face, but his goggled headset kept his vision clear. The beast seemed to be carrying some sort of howdah, upon which stood three or four dark-green bipedal shapes. There were guns, too. Lots of them, welded to the howdah rails. Whoever the shapes were, they seemed not to notice him.

Omega tried his best to angle himself into a trajectory that followed their descent. The jungle was sickeningly close now, an enormous leafy ocean that he couldn't miss. He started his search for a safe landing but found that his speed negated every potential. It was time, he deemed, to hope for the best.

As he hurtled into the giant net of trees, Omega pulled his feet in beneath him. The heel rockets kicked off just as he'd intended, slowing him somewhat. The first two big branches were not as painful as he had guessed, but the third and subsequent ones hurt much, much more. Omega found himself battered, spun around, and then, inexplicably, motionless. He was lying on his back without any clear memory of stopping—a sure sign of a blackout.

As his headset came back online, Omega checked his vital signs. His gear still seemed more or less intact, the sensors in his patch-work flight suit giving better than expected news. While it did mention that his body was likely to swell into one gigantic bruise sometime within a day or so, it reported no serious hemorrhaging and only one broken bone. His left leg, it seemed, was pretty thoroughly shattered below the knee. Less encouraging was the fact that his heads-up display was informing him of moving objects close by.

The pain in his leg threatened to put him out, but Omega focused on the jungle. He had fallen pretty far, by the looks of things. The branch which had finally stopped him was a bit wider than a kitchen table, and much thicker than the limbs that grew near the canopy. The light from above was minimal. What little came through cast the jungle in an almost gothic atmosphere, the branches and trunks becoming the huge pillars of some primordial church. And the insects. Great Gods of Harmony, the insects were everywhere. Thousands of them, in the air, on the tree trunks, even on the branches around him.

He heard a cracking, crumbling sound. Before him, a knothole in the trunk had begun vomiting out veiny, sticky-looking grubs the size of small house pets. From what he could see, the awful white invertebrates had neither a front nor a back end. They began moving in every direction. Several tumbled off the side of the branch, and a few even seemed to be heading back the way they'd come. Most, though, had begun to writhe his way. Whichever end was facing him, it had two or three nail-shaped prongs that the critters used to drag themselves along. Omega wasn't rightly sure what they were going to do with him, but now, at least, he knew which end to aim for.

He unhooked the clasp that held his ray-gun in its holster and proceeded to nearly drop the thing as he tried to roll over. It was good, he thought, that his leg was still cracked. If this got too easy now, he'd likely start to lose his edge. Trying the maneuver again with a little less speed, Omega got himself around just in time for a grub to move within swatting range. The little creep actually reared half of its body in the air as a threat.

"Good move," Omega acknowledged, through gritted teeth. "My turn?"

The ray-gun whined as it fired, superheating the already humid air, exploding the grub. Guts spattered against his face and hands, and oozed across the tree limb. The others seemed not to take any notice, though, and, as each of them continued wriggling forward, Omega realized that he was likely to become literal worms' meat if he didn't do something quickly. Unfortunately, doing anything quickly at this point was a very difficult venture. Jaw clenched, ray-gun blazing, Omega swallowed the pain shooting up his leg and began forcing himself farther out on the limb.

The branch began to shake. Omega tried to steady it by stopping, but nothing changed. It intensified instead, flinging the grubs in every direction. The pain in his leg made his vision swim. Despite this, he could hear a scraping sound.

As the last of the monstrosities fell over the edge, he could just make out what looked like a handful of curved sticks poking out from the knothole. The shaking subsided, but the sticks in the knothole were moving frantically now. Like tiny grappling hooks, they were pulling away bits of the tree. As it eroded, Omega could make out what looked to be a set of bulbous eyes surrounded by chitinous armour plates.

With one fantastic rip, the thing tore through the tree trunk. It had countless legs and awful, spiny hairs across it back. Delicate feelers feeding sharp, clacking mandibles. Cold, dead eyes staring out from an insectoid head.

"This is not better," Omega said. No wonder the little grubs had been so frantic. The thing that had crawled from the tree hissed and then surged forward.

It didn't make it within a foot of him.

Just as Omega levelled his gun, a hulking green figure crashed down through the branches above. The monstrous centipede barely had time to register its assailant before it was struck down, a massive sword pinning it through the head. As the creature's body stopped spasming, Omega examined his rescuer.

The creature was dappled green and brown. As it crouched over its trophy, he could see taught biceps bulging beneath scaly skin and a broad set of shoulders. Its head was distinctly reptilian. Omega could see a boxy snout and glittering amber eyes. His headset scanners could only interpret some of its vital organs, but found enough to identify the creature as female.

She was watching him in return now, standing on thick, tridactyl legs, her waist and right shoulder covered by a toga of animal hides. A sprawling length of tail uncoiled behind her. The humanoid reptile yanked its sword free and hefted it across one shoulder.

Omega grimaced as he offered his best charming smile, re-positioning his ray-gun as he did so. He was making ready to fire when his headset abruptly registered a large incoming body. The foliage above began to shake vigorously, and a massive woolly shape descended the trunk.

This new creature looked something like a rodent with wings, and Omega recognized it as the beast that had flown past him during his fall. The howdah on its back held three more reptilian aliens. He could see now that the whole thing was covered in rails and handholds that the reptiles used to keep from falling out.

His rescuer began to communicate with the others in the howdah. It was impossible to tell what the stream of hisses and clicks happening between them actually meant, but their vigorous gestures certainly implied they were speaking about him. One of the reptiles reached into a compartment Omega couldn't see and threw two small objects to his saviour. The alien applied one of the devices to the side of her head, then held the other mechanism up for Omega to see.

"Right. I get it." Omega pointed at his ear and motioned for the device. He found it was too cumbersome for him to put on as the alien did, especially with his own headset attached, but he clipped it haphazardly to his own headgear, nonetheless. "Will it calibrate to my language if it hears me speak?"

"Yes, exactly," she affirmed as the machine translated her reptilian vocalizations into Basic.

"What does it say?" asked one of her male comrades from the howdah.

"It displays basic intelligence despite its obviously primitive biology. See how quickly I have trained it to use our translators?"

"No special training required actually," Omega cut in. "The concept is pretty obvious. Not that I'm not grateful bu—" He winced as the throbbing in his leg reasserted itself.

"It is injured. Look at the heat rising from its lower leg," assessed a reptile in the howdah.

"Yes, I can see that." The translator did little to convey tone, but Omega could tell his rescuer was irritated. "Your comments are not helpful. Throw me a brace." Another piece of equipment was tossed to his rescuer. This time she approached him.

"Do not fear. This will help." She crouched above him. Omega could feel her gently attaching the equipment to his leg, just below the knee. When she had finished, she pressed a button. Omega stifled a scream as the device clamped down. "The brace will hold the bones steady while the radiation pack speeds the healing process. Lie still for a few moments, my pet, and you will soon walk with less pain.

"I am called Hoonra" — this was the best Omega could interpret from the sounds the translator made in his ear — "but you will refer to me as Master."

Before Omega could say anything, Hoonra turned to her companions on the howdah. "The karnax is slain, and the hunt is successful. I leave its carcass to the jungle; instead, I claim this creature as my trophy."

Omega's mouth went a little dry. In the howdah, Hoonra's companions spoke quietly to each other.

"You are not yet old enough to train a mammal, Hoonra. They require much work and attention."

"I am nobody's pet," said Omega.

"Be silent, pet," said Hoonra, turning back to her companions. "I am well within my rights, Rokan." More guttural buzzing from the translator. "The mammal is mine."

"This is very unorthodox. You are still in the process of completing your coming-of-age ceremony. It shall not be."

"It shall," argued Hoonra, stamping her foot.

"Harmony save me, I'm being adopted by a teenager," Omega groaned.

"Hush, pet. I name you Hairy, because you are." Without eyebrows or lips it was hard to read anything on her face, but Omega got the distinct impression that Hoonra was pleased with herself. Rokan, alternatively, was not.

"Mammals are not toys, Hoonra. This discussion is not over. We will take him back with us and decide what should be done with him on Karackas." Two more of the lizard-like aliens jumped out of the howdah and approached, sweeping past Hoonra even as she protested.

Omega scurried backwards on the branch. When he realized his leg was, in fact, healing as Hoonra said it would, he stood up, edging himself away from the lizard folk and out towards the canopy.

"Stop it. You are scaring him," Hoonra pleaded.

The two aliens stalked forward, and Omega could see them considering the ray-gun in his hand. He waved it back and forth a little. "You're wondering what this is, I guess. Glad you noticed."

Without taking his eyes from them, he angled the weapon above their heads. As he fired, he flicked his wrist, cutting a small swatch of foliage from above, which promptly fell on the encroaching aliens. The whine of the ray-gun arrested their attention, and they leapt back in surprise as the branches and leaves fell down around them. Hoonra and Rokan ceased bickering, everyone now staring at Omega. He gave them a showman's grin.

"I know, right? I find a little controlled gunfire to be a fantastic way of getting people's attention. You shouldn't be that surprised, though. Maybe you haven't seen this particular model before, but you definitely brought your own." He motioned towards the armaments hanging from the howdah.

"You see, Hoonra, the mammal's ignorance is dangerous." Rokan turned to address Omega for the first time. "Such weapons are a coward's tool. I see the blade on your hip. Have you no honour, mammal? We hunt with sword and strength. Beam weaponry is only a last defence."

"Sure, last defence. Like when you shot my bird out of the sky on your way here?"

Rokan shook his head. "Impossible. We shot only at the scavenger vessel, who attacked us first."

Ah, thought Omega, now we're getting somewhere. "Alright, so tell me about these scavengers."

"What is there to say?" Rokan shrugged, "They are like you: mammals, ignorant and violent. They hide in orbit around our home and profit by stealing the wealth of others. They have no honour."

"And what have they stolen from you?"

"Little enough, Hairy," Hoonra chimed in. "Our settlements are well-defended, and the scavengers flee into deeper space at the first sign of organized resistance. Their shots at us earlier were meant to cover a retreat."

That made sense, given how wild the barrage of fire had been. Omega nodded, holstering his weapon. Time, it seemed, to try making friends instead.

"I'm going to have to be honest with you, Hoonra. I'm really not all that interested in becoming your pet. But this leaves you with a problem, right? Without me, you have no prize for your hunt."

Before Hoonra could answer, Rokan snorted, "It's not a problem for us, mammal. Hoonra could complete her trial just as easily by hunting you."

Omega waited for some hint of sarcasm to register in his voice. There was nothing. Still, no going back now. "Oddly enough, Rokan, I've got an idea about that."

Ω

As the late night air pelted against the open face of the howdah, Omega turned back to Hoonra. "Tell me again how you folks manage to fly these things through space."

"Certainly, Omega." It had taken some doing, but he'd finally managed to get her to use his actual name. "Krildar and Karackas share an atmosphere. They are locked in a special, synchronous orbit, and are so close we can fly between them. It is not easy."

Omega thought that was likely an understatement. It wasn't that he didn't understand the concept. It was just that any time he

11

imagined flying nearly into the vacuum of space in what amounted to a steel backpack strapped to a gigantic flying rat, he felt deeply sick.

"It is all part of the ritual of the hunt. Only the best of us may become hunters."

"Yeah, I guess so. And this was meant to be your initiation, right? Like, some sort of coming-of-age thing?"

"Yes, something like that."

"Well, I'm sure that your folks — uh, your parents, I mean — must be very proud."

Hoonra looked at him, her brow furrowing in puzzlement. "You are attempting a compliment? It is kind, but misguided. We have no special bonds to our progenitors. We are born in clutches, hatched and trained for our roles from birth. I have been training to become a hunter all my life."

"All your life, huh? I hope you don't mind my asking, but since I'm being educated anyway, how long would that be?"

Hoonra cocked her head. "We pay little attention to the conventions of the wider galaxy, so my counting may be a bit off. Still, you could say that I'm one hundred and eighty-seven Standard Years old."

"Seriously?"

"Yes. Why?"

"We are approaching their base," Rokan called back to them. Despite Omega's proposed solution, Rokan's attitude towards him had not improved.

Omega peered over the side of the howdah, scanning with his headset, and decided that "base" might be too strong a word. Below, set amongst the foliage, he could see a camp passing beneath them. A series of canvas-covered huts and camouflage projectors had been erected around a makeshift landing platform. Temporary steel walkways snaked their way out from this central point to hang among the trees. This was the staging ground for getting their stolen resources off-planet.

The platform itself was still empty, and Omega wondered how long before the scavengers would try another landing. Probably not at all until they were sure Rokan's hunters had left again. Sentries had been placed in a few obvious locations around the perimeter, but the site looked otherwise lightly defended. This was not a surprise. These raiders had been operating under the governing Corporation's nose for quite a while. Likely, they thought they were past any serious retribution. Looking up, Omega saw Rokan motioning him to the front of the carrier.

"Doesn't look like they're expecting anybody," Omega said, awkwardly pulling himself forward on rungs and catches that were clearly not designed for human proportions.

"No, and why should they? My people have no interest in them." Rokan sniffed as he hauled on the reins that controlled their ride. "Their laxity is a boon for you. I would expect few others."

"What do you mean?" Omega asked.

"This was your idea," Rokan sneered. "You wished to save Hoonra's honour and your employer's supplies. So be it. But the rest of us will not accompany you."

"Why? You don't think this will work?"

"Certainly, it will, though it is unnecessary. Hoonra, at least, will be fine; she killed the karnax and other beasts besides. You, on the other hand, are simple prey." Rokan turned to regard him. "Hoonra's attachment to you is typical of a child. She will lose it once she is faced with your incompetence."

Omega's face flushed. Rokan held his gaze for a moment longer, and Omega had the distinct impression the alien knew exactly what was going through his mind. Abruptly, Rokan turned his back. "We land south of their location shortly. Be ready."

Omega made his way to the back of the howdah.

"Rokan does not like you," Hoonra said.

"You heard all that?"

"No. I do not need to. We can see body heat. You turned very bright towards the end." She made a hissing, hiccupping sound that Omega assumed to be laughter. "You still are. Besides, Rokan does not like anything, especially if it involves outsiders and breaking traditions. There are many people like him back home. Do not worry about it. I think this is a good idea. The galaxy is a wide place; I have always thought of seeing more of it. Just remember" — Hoonra reached over, tapping the hilt of his pulsword — "we fight first with honour."

"Right." Omega sucked his teeth. Hoonra seemed pleased enough, and he was getting what he wanted out of the deal. No point in counting scores just yet. He tucked Rokan's words away. There would be time for that later.

Their flyer had begun to descend, dropping through the night sky in complete silence. It landed among the top branches and crawled down towards the trunk. Omega could see the light of the not-so-distant camp as the world began to move vertically past him. He clung to the rails on the side, hooking his feet under the rails on the floor. The creature they were riding managed not to travel straight down, instead passing the tiers branch by branch. Soon, they leveled out and stopped.

Rokan stood. Silently, he pointed into the trees, outlining the general direction of the camp. Hoonra stood, pulling herself over the rail and falling quietly to the branch below. Omega followed, ignoring the look Rokan sent after him. The drop wasn't far and, though he wasn't able to move with quite her stealth, Omega had soon caught up with his scaled companion.

The Lizardwoman led the way through the undergrowth. Despite her bulk, Hoonra moved with the assurance of a trained predator. Omega found that he had to work to keep pace.

While he followed, Omega mused on just how often in his life he had found himself face to face with a creature he'd never encountered before. In these situations, hostility was, as often as not, the focus of the meeting. In light of this, Omega found himself happy that, for once, the gigantic, fang-toothed, snap-you-like-a-twig warrior was on his side.

Hoonra stopped mid-step just ahead of him, and Omega nearly crashed into her back. She pointed and, peering over her shoulder, he could make out one of the metal walkways. He reached back, unsheathing his pulsword, but Hoonra stopped him as he began to move forward.

"What is it?" he whispered.

"What are we doing?"

"What? What do you mean? We're going to go in there and mash these raiders."

Hoonra shook her head. "We are hunters. I know how to hunt a karnax. How do we hunt these 'thugs', as you say? What is our strategy?"

Omega chewed his lip for a moment. "You know, Hoonra, if I'm being honest, I don't know if I've ever really thought about it like that. Normally, I just sort of start swinging. I've found that, as far as functionality goes, that's about as much as any plan ever delivers on anyways." Before Hoonra could respond, Omega pushed past her and onto the walkway.

The foliage from his vantage point on the branch had been dense. Omega figured this was likely the reason he hadn't seen the small troop of guards approaching below him until he dropped fully into plain sight. The foremost of them seemed particularly unimpressed.

"Just who the hell are you?" the lead guard asked, reaching for his gun.

"Hey there," Omega replied brightly, before slamming the pommel of his pulsword into the guard's mouth. The man's teeth made a gravelly, crunching noise, and gave Omega a grim sense of satisfaction. The pulsword was designed to deliver localized electromagnetic pulses on impact, disabling things like personal shields, but Omega found that it worked just as well the old-fashioned way too. As the guard began howling, Omega pulled back, round-housing his crossguard into the side of the unfortunate fellow's jaw. There was a popping sound and the man crumpled. The other three guards had gone pale.

"Hey, listen guys" — Omega hoped he sounded charming — "I can explain about that—"

"Gods of Entropy, look at it," whispered the guard in the centre.

"Huh?" Omega regarded their friend. "Oh, yeah, you're right. That was awful of me. I kind of panicked, you know? I mean, he's probably going to have to eat through a straw for—" He bit off the last few words as Hoonra rushed past him. Like a green boulder, she barrelled into the three men, scattering them. She reached out, catching one of the guards by the back of his collar. Muscles bulging, she hefted the man in an over-the-shoulder arc, hurling him off the ramp and into the jungle depths. She whipped her tail about herself as he fell, letting it snap out at another of the men. The force of it slung him sideways, dropping him to the walkway. Omega could hear his bones cracking with the impact.

Meanwhile, Hoonra had completed her spin. With a flourish, she whirled her blade above her head before sending the point downward into the back of the last scavenger. She held it there for just a moment before twisting it viciously and withdrawing it. She turned to Omega.

"Wow," he said.

"Really? You're impressed?"

"Oh yeah. Truly. That was fantastic."

"Well, I did say I'd been training all my life." Hoonra was clearly pleased with the compliment.

"No, I know. It shows. I mean that would have taken me, probably fifteen or twenty minutes to do on my own. You were like an avalanche. Do all of your people fight like that?" Omega began searching the fallen guards.

"Our warriors do, yes. What are you looking for?"

"These." Omega held up a few palm-sized cylinders attached to a belt.

Hoonra's eyes widened. "I know what those are. We cannot. There is no honour in this."

"Look, Hoonra" — Omega slung the belt across his shoulder — "I hear what you're saying about honour, I really do." He gestured with his pulsword. "I'm happy using this thing, but hear me out. You asked what my plan was. The truth is, I improvise. It's basically my area of expertise." He patted the cylinders. "These are what you call an *opportunity*.

"Now, I understand that you're probably more than happy taking down each and every one of these raiders with your bare hands, but I also understand that even if you do, their setup is still going to be here. Others are eventually going to find it, and then the people who hired me are going to be in exactly the same position they are right now.

"We've got to cripple the operation here permanently, but we also need to give these goons something to think about. That's going to require a little extra 'oomph', you know what I'm saying? Besides, I require satisfaction."

"Satisfaction?"

"They shot my bird, Hoonra," Omega said, a little more forcefully than he'd meant to. "That was a damn loyal pterosaur. I even built a nest for it on my ship. I've been here for weeks looking for these creeps, and the first sign I actually find of them, they shoot my bird."

Hoonra nodded and moved towards him. Gently, she placed her massive hand on his shoulder. "I understand, Omega. I, too, have recently lost a new pet." Again, that hissing, hiccupping sound.

Omega shrugged her away, scowling. "You need to work on your comedic timing. Let's get this over with."

The pair jogged down the catwalk. The overhanging foliage became less dense as they moved, and the light from the lamps was bright. Better to move quickly, then. Omega could see they were coming to the big junction in the middle.

"There you are," he said, as he came off the catwalk. Before him sat two small fuel tanks set to the side of the landing zone. "Just buy me a minute or two, all right?" he called over his shoulder as he approached the tanks. "This won't take long." Omega lay on his stomach, pushing the grenades under the tank supports as he did so.

"Buy you a minute?" Hoonra asked.

"It means 'stand guard'." Even as he said it, Omega was interrupted by a klaxon's wail. Scanning the platform, he could see boots scurrying back and forth at the far end of the landing pad. "Behind you!" he called, realizing as he did it that he could no longer see where his companion had gone.

Omega turned his attention back to the grenades, looping and knotting the belt around the struts that supported the tanks. These ones had been a particularly good find, owing to the timers attached to their detonators. He was keying them all for two minutes when he heard the boots getting closer.

The feet from the other side of the platform had, apparently, decided to get close and drag him out rather than risk a stray shot at the tanks. He could hear more coming from behind him as well, which was fine, except that the alien bodyguard he'd brought was gone, and the dial on the second grenade was loose and, even if he got it working now, they'd all still be standing right beside it when the damn things went off, and where the hell had Hoonra—

There was a crash to his immediate right, followed by screaming. Omega could see two enormous reptilian legs striding through the group of uniforms and boots. As he watched, the guards began scrambling. Several were lifted bodily from the platform, while others were slashed open by the Karackian's sword.

Omega waited until the nearest raiders were fully taken care of before finishing with the last grenade. He scrambled out from beneath the tanks and stood, surveying the sheer depth of Hoonra's handiwork.

"Yeah. Again, super-impressive. I'm a total fan of your work. We should probably go now, though." He started running down the catwalk they had taken to reach the platform, Hoonra close behind. He looked back as they neared the place where they'd arrived.

"Nobody seems too keen on following us."

"There looked to be a fair number of the scavengers coming from one of the larger tents. I threw one of their colleagues through the side of that shelter to slow them down. I believe I frightened them."

"No kidding? Hoonra, would I be correct in assuming that you can run quite a bit faster than I can?"

"Yes."

"Right, then this is where we split up for a little bit." Omega reached down and activated his boots. The little jets lifted him a foot or so in the air. "We don't want to be this close when those tanks blow. Head back to Rokan, I'll meet you there."

Hoonra nodded and then disappeared into the jungle. Omega keyed the boots with his headset and took off. He hadn't flown more than twenty seconds before the explosion happened. The blast had a less shattering effect on the surrounding area than Omega had thought. Still, he had to compensate in-flight as the shockwave rolled past him. His helmet located Rokan and his flying mammal. The branches were still swaying when he landed.

Hoonra had managed to arrive first, just as she'd said. She was standing toe to toe with Rokan, and Omega could hear the two saurians growling and hissing at each other. The other two aliens kept a healthy distance. Omega's headset was having a bit of a problem keeping up, but he didn't need a translator to tell him he was watching an argument.

"It had to be done, Rokan," Hoonra insisted as he approached.

"Nonsense," the older lizard fired back. He pointed over her shoulder at Omega. "He has convinced you to commit this...this transgression."

Given the look he saw in Rokan's eyes, Omega thought it best to stay a few feet back, keeping Hoonra between them.

"He did not need to convince me. It was the most effective way to deal with the scavengers quickly and permanently."

"But honour demands—"

"Hoonra did fight with honour," Omega interjected. "She used only her steel and her bare hands. I was the one who cheated." He put on a grim smile. "It was the only way prey like me could have survived." He could hear Rokan growling deep in his throat, which was exactly the kind of thoroughly angry noise he'd been hoping for. Time to play his last card.

"Either way, what's done is done now—though there's still the matter of payment to be considered."

As if on cue, Rokan bellowed. Sudden as a striking snake, he leapt towards Omega. There was nothing he could have done to stop the colossal lizard, and it was only his good luck that Hoonra kept working to stand between them.

"We owe you nothing!" Rokan spat between bared fangs.

"No, of course not," Omega replied. "You know, Rokan, for the one in charge, you don't come across as all that smart." The Lizardman's eyes bulged slightly, and Omega continued: "No, I wasn't asking for credit. I was offering."

"We want nothing from you," hissed Rokan.

Omega nodded. "Well then, it's a handy thing I wasn't offering it to you. I'm offering it to her."

Hoonra turned as he spoke. "What do you mean?"

"Well, remember I told you that I was being paid to take care of those scavengers? They're gone now, and I'll be getting that payment in full. But I'm not the one who did most of the hard work. In fact, looking back, it seems like you did almost all of the heavy lifting, Hoonra, which means that you should get a chunk of the pay. After all," he looked back at Rokan, "it would be the honourable thing for me to do."

Rokan straightened, his expression becoming bored. "Stupidity, as usual. What use would Hoonra have for your off-world currency on Karackas?"

"Not very much, I guess. That's why I would encourage her not to go back there. Lots of opportunity to make currency and spend it, if she's travelling the galaxy working with me as my bodyguard instead." Omega held out his hand. "What do you say, Hoonra? You mentioned that you wanted to see more of the galaxy. Here's your chance."

Hoonra regarded Omega for a moment. "Truly?" she asked. Her pupils dilated, and Omega's headset told him her heart rate had shot up. She was, he supposed, excited by the offer.

Instead of taking his hand, she grabbed him by the shoulders, pulling him into a massive hug. Even her tail curled around him, and Omega could feel his ribs straining to maintain their shape within his chest.

"On Karackas, this is how we express agreement among close friends. I would love to accompany you, Omega. Consider me as your bodyguard," she said.

"Swell," Omega wheezed.

"Absolutely not!" shouted Rokan. The alien was so irate that Omega could see the tone of his skin slipping into a bright red even in the predawn light. "The words of outsiders are like sand on a beach. You will hear me when I—"

Hoonra dropped Omega onto the branch and spun around. With one solid push, she heaved Rokan onto his back. Omega couldn't decide if Rokan looked more full of surprise or blind rage.

"No, Rokan" — Hoonra overrode her elder when he tried to speak — "*You* will hear *me*. I have passed the ritual today, twice now, and I am an adult by every standard our people hold, whether you will acknowledge it or not. As an adult I choose my own path. Omega is unorthodox, but he is honourable. I will follow him and see what this galaxy has to show me. You have no say in this. Goodbye, Rokan." Hoonra did not even look at the two aliens still in the howdah; she turned her back and moved towards another tree.

Rokan stood, glowering. It was clear to Omega that things had turned decidedly off-course as far as the Karackian was concerned, and this was likely his best chance to leave with all of his limbs still attached. "See you around, Rokan."

"Pray that you do not." Rokan's voice quivered a little, and Omega had to force himself not to walk faster. "Do not ever show your face here again, or anywhere else I can find it, or you will live to regret it."

"Yeah," Omega muttered, "that's what they all say." He jumped down to a wide branch growing out of a different tree. When he reached the trunk, he found Hoonra waiting for him. She stood with her arms crossed, her head tilted to the side, listening. Faintly, Omega could hear the soft beating of leathery wings gaining altitude.

"So, any regrets? I got a real rush out of annoying Tall, Green, and Ugly like that, but I bet we can still figure out a way for you to get back to Karackas, if that's what you want."

Hoonra shook her head. "No. I am tired of the rigidity of my home. It is time for me to move on and see what I can find elsewhere." She motioned to the jungle around them. "Where are we going now?"

"Now?" Omega looked at his wrist comp and activated the homing beacon. "Well, first we're going to go clean up my campsite. Then, we're going to get back on my ship and collect our payment. After that?" He shrugged. "After that, we see just how much trouble we can get ourselves into."

Episode 2:

The Tellarian Shapeshifter

Looking back on it, Omega wasn't really sure which of his answers had enraged the pirates more. Refusing their demands to accept a boarding party would have been upsetting, he supposed, but if Omega had to choose, he'd place his bet on it being his comments about the captain's mother. Regardless, there wasn't much point in dwelling on it. So long as he managed to avoid being vaporized, he'd call the patrol trip a victory.

Omega leaned forward in his seat, coaxing more speed from the *Buccaneer's* engines, rolling the ship between laser blasts as he went. From somewhere in the hold, he heard a loud thump.

"Some warning would be welcome before you try that again," shouted his bodyguard.

"Gods of Harmony, Hoonra, are you not strapped into the gun turret yet?"

"You did not mention anything about the—"

"Now is really not the time for this. If we're getting shot at, you can safely assume I want you in the turret."

The *Buccaneer's* hull shuddered in agreement. Even with Hoonra at the guns, things were beginning to look tight. Staying fully out of their enemy's sights was becoming an increasingly difficult chore.

The onboard systems panel flashed, and Omega could see Hoonra had powered up the guns. His sensors reported the pirate vessel moving suddenly back. It was good to catch them off guard, but he doubted it would last. If the pirates were no longer chasing, now was likely the best opportunity to run.

The governing Corporation in charge of this sector had asked him to scout for pirate activity across their lesser-travelled trade routes. The solar system they'd been cruising through was backwater, the planets unexplored, as far as he knew. Omega decided it was time to change that precedent. In particular, the closest planet, the one covered by swirling grey storm clouds, seemed like the most expedient option.

"Are you certain this is the best choice?" The intercom buzzed beside him.

"Hoonra, what did we agree on?"

"You told me to stop questioning your improvisations. I did not agree to anything."

"How about we talk it over after the landing?"

The planet was far closer now, its grey cloud cover giving way to tones of bruised purple and sudden blue lightning. Omega reconsidered his copilot's wisdom, but his ship's sensors informed him that his pursuers were back and gaining. A bright orange warning light informed him that they had locked onto the *Buccaneer* with missiles. He flicked the intercom back on.

"Get out of the turret, Hoonra."

"You just told me to get in it."

"Well, now I'm telling you to get out. Come back up and buckle yourself in. The next few minutes are going to be pretty unpleasant." He could hear her grumbling in Karackian as she started her ascent. Among the many things she'd proven adept at learning, languages were near the top of the list. Omega was pretty sure she only bothered to speak her own in his earshot when she was cussing him out.

They entered the upper atmosphere, and immediately turbulence began affecting the ship. As Omega pushed into the first cloud bank, the *Buccaneer* informed him that the pirates had fired their missiles. Both ships were hurtling through the storm now, the missiles struggling to follow their target amidst the turmoil outside.

Truth be told, Omega was struggling a little himself. He leaned over the intercom once more. "Hoonra, I don't know where you are but if you haven't—"

His words were cut short as one of the missiles found its target. The *Buccaneer* heaved and began to spin. Before him, Omega could see the dark brown of a soaked landscape circling wildly beneath. He was just righting his ship when the second missile destroyed his primary engine. Flaming, debris flying in all directions as it fell, the *Buccaneer* hurtled towards the planet's surface

Ω

After the surface of the planet, the second thing that struck Omega was the headache. It seeped down from the crown of his skull and trickled its way across his neck and back, soaking through the whole of his nervous system. The third thing that struck him was the garbage. It wasn't the smell—though that certainly was omnipresent— so much as the sheer quantity of it all.

While the *Buccaneer* had been falling, Omega had seen what he had taken to be a field of irregularly-shaped rock outcroppings. In actuality, they were piles of starship wreckage, and heaps bigger than his ship filled his view of the horizon. He eased his head back against the seat and closed his eyes.

"Omega?" He jerked and then winced. Opening one eye a slit, he could see Hoonra's concerned bulk bent over him.

"I'll never get used to how quiet you are."

"Are you all right?"

He touched the bandage around his head. "You tell me."

"You certainly were not for a while there. The bandage comes from your shirt. There was not anything else at hand. Omega, the *Buccaneer* is destroyed."

"Yeah, tell me another one. What happened? I remember the first explosion, but nothing else."

Hoonra brushed shattered chunks of console from the seat beside him and sat down. "Well, I do not know everything, but I can guess. For a start, you were the one who landed us, more or less. It is how you hit your head. Obviously, we were coming in too fast; I assume that the terrain tore most of our landing equipment out as we skidded through."

"I landed us, eh? And whenabouts did I perform this miracle?"

"That was two days ago."

Omega lurched up at this, then groaned and fell back. "What about the pirates?" he asked, when his head had settled.

"No sign, which I take to mean they are either dead or in worse shape than we are. It is hardly as if we lost them. Anybody could have seen the wreck we made from the ground, let alone flying right behind us. Since our crash, I have been outside surveying the damage. Given how much of the engine appears to be missing, it's likely the *Buccaneer* took them out with her debris. Their sensors would have been just as dead as ours on the way down." Hoonra patted what was left of the console. "A fine ship, she was. A fighter."

"A pile of garbage more like." Omega didn't try to hide the bitterness he felt. "Not that I'm not grateful, Hoonra, but how did you manage not to get hurt?"

"I have always been lucky. Also, when we entered the atmosphere, I rethought what you said about strapping myself in. Very occasionally, your tactical appraisals are spot-on accurate."

Omega gave a weak shrug. "I was due," he sighed. "So what now? Are we stranded here till someone else crashes? I mean, then, of course, we'll still be stranded, we'll just have more company."

"When I first found you, I was too worried to move you, but now that you are awake, things are different. Can you sit forward?" He did so, the effort clearly a strain. Hoonra pointed out the cockpit window.

They didn't stick out to him at first, their clothes too close in colour to the junk around them. Still after a moment of searching, he could see four humanoid shapes dressed in mottled rags.

"No pirates, Omega, but as I said before, it has been two days since the crash. In the time you slept, there have been some developments."

Ω

Omega's headache was gone. He felt fine. Actually, he felt better than fine. He felt so refreshed, in fact, that it took him a few moments to register where he was.

The room he lay in was dark, save for a single light which bobbed somewhere in the shadows above his head. He couldn't see any wires connecting to the ceiling. He couldn't, as he strained, see the ceiling at all. The dimensions of the room escaped him, the floor beneath stretching out into a gloom his eyes felt too weak to penetrate.

He sat up, searching with his fingers for the surface he'd lain upon. He felt nothing beneath him and, as he groped down further, felt a jolt as he realized that he'd actually been standing the whole time.

"Where am I?" he asked, searching the ground behind him.

"Do you feel better?"

Omega jumped, shouting a little, and spun back in the direction he'd been facing. A human girl stood before him now. He had no idea how he'd missed her the first time. She stood about half his height, her head covered in flowing blonde curls which reached down to a dark purple dress that swept over her shoulders, and then cascaded down to the floor. Her bearing was authoritative but disquieting, owing to her mismatched eyes: one orb white, the other totally black.

"Who are you? Kid, you scared the hell out of me."

"Do you feel better?" She spoke as if she hadn't heard him.

Omega rubbed his head. "Yeah, I guess I do."

"Then you can help us?"

"Help us? Who's us? Kid, who are you?" Omega looked around the room. "I don't even know where *I* am right now."

The girl's voice was louder this time, making his head snap back to her. "You have to help us," she said, and it was then that he saw her mouth wasn't moving. "You have to. You have to!" As her voice grew louder, she stomped her feet beneath the shapeless flow of her gown. "You have to! You have to! You—"

"No!" Omega yelled.

"No what?" Hoonra asked.

Omega looked around once more. The dim room he had seen was now replaced by the makings of a healing centre. It wasn't big, holding only five cots aside from his. The walls here were clearly visible, and obviously made from the junk strewn across the rest of the planet. Scavenged glass windows lined one wall of the centre, but the light that filtered in was dim. One end of the room was punctuated by a door of the old manual variety.

At the other end, against the back wall of the enclosure, were the smooth white lines and sloping angles of some sort of giant incubator. The thing itself was running, plugged into various cables which disappeared into the wall, and Omega noted that it looked nothing like the rest of the cobbled-together equipment filling the room.

Standing, testing his legs and balance, Omega approached. "Sorry, I had a weird dream. What is that? It's the only thing in here with any cables."

"Indeed." Hoonra was only a step behind. "Strange that they would keep a medical centre yet limit any access to electricity. But if you think the object is odd, Omega, you should look inside."

The viewer was foggy, and Omega could feel the heat rising from the glass when he leaned over. The condensation made it difficult to discern the form swaddled within. He leaned closer, staring into the sepia-lit chamber. He could make out very little of what he saw until he finally noticed the eyes. Totally familiar. One black, the other white. Omega recoiled in shock, then peered in again.

The eyes were motionless and vacant, unlike in his dream. He could make out the nose now, and even the drooling crease of the mouth beneath. Above the eyes, a cranium ballooned outwards, covered in thick dark veins and a few scant wisps of blond hair.

The head was massive, more than twice the size of the feeble body wrapped up beneath it. Sensors surrounded the skull, blinking periodically, and a variety of tubes and wires were tucked into the swaddle at the opposite end.

"Hey kid," Omega whispered.

"You know it?"

"Her. And no, I don't. Not really. Just now, when I was on that bed, I had a dream. A little girl with eyes just like those spoke to me. Told me that the people here needed help. It's funny, but normally I can hardly remember my dreams."

"The Dreamer's visions are always clear, always memorable," said a voice from the door. It spoke a form of galactic Basic, though an odd variation, and Omega had to adjust his headset for a translation. The pair turned to see a blue-skinned humanoid dressed in the brown and grey robes Omega remembered from the wreck of his ship. "And she meant what she said. We do need your help."

"You seem to understand me well enough."

The man nodded. "We've spent the last few days in conversation with your guardian. I'm becoming more used to your dialect."

"Who's we?" Omega found he was becoming tired of asking that.

"We are the Disciples, the Faithful of the One Dream." The blue-skinned man bowed as he spoke, jingling the bits of metal pierced through the fins on his head.

"That's interesting but, unless you want me to refer to you as a whole gathering, you're going to have to give me something specific."

The man looked back up with the beginnings of a scowl. "I am called Ennis. I am the Avatar; our Lady speaks to the congregation through me. The Dreamer wanted us to heal you, and now it is time for you to pay your debts."

Omega crossed his arms. "I don't remember asking for your help."

Ennis shrugged. "More to the point, you never told us that you preferred death either. An attitude, I believe, you still hold?" Omega could feel Hoonra tense beside him.

"Threatening your guests," she said, "is not usually a good way to gain their trust."

"No indeed. That is why the Dreamer wishes to make you an offer."

Omega and Hoonra traded glances. The Karackian relaxed and Omega resumed the lead. "What did you have in mind?"

"Your ship has lost much of its integrity, yet many of the more" — Ennis searched for the right words — "*volatile* elements remain intact."

"Ennis, again, you're need to be more specific."

Hoonra leaned back in. "I think he means the fuel, Omega."

"Stop making his job easier. I'll talk; you be the muscle."

"Your companion is correct, however," Ennis interrupted. "And to be, as you say, specific—I mean your warp core. We have been here a long time, Omega Brown. Generations. The ships of our ancestors crashed on Tellaria much as yours did. As many have. Our progenitors survived because they heard and served the One Dream, protected her even as they fell. We can build a ship. There are parts aplenty. We've even managed to generate limited amounts of electricity. What we can't do is create new fuel, much less a way to break the barrier to warp space."

"So, we let you use our frame and our fuel, you repair the ship, and then what, we all leave here together?"

"Yes. For transportation away from this planet and system, you can consider your life debt paid."

"And how do we win back the ship?" Hoonra interjected.

"Hoonra, I swear, I'm going to leave you here if—" He stopped when he noticed the intensity in the Karackian's eyes. "Ennis, does Hoonra know something I don't?"

"Perhaps your bodyguard should be made into a negotiator." The blue humanoid did little to hide his contempt. "She pays more attention than you do. Certainly, she's better at bargaining."

"And why would I have to win back my own ship?'

"What ship? By the time we're done with it, the machine will be mostly comprised of our parts. We are clever. We can still build quite a bit, even if we have lost our forefathers' expertise. What we need is a pilot, and you are the only one around."

Omega could feel his face getting red, but Ennis continued before he could speak. "We would be happy to give it back to you, of course—for a price."

"Which is?"

"There is another task." Ennis turned and opened the door. "It will be easier if I show you." He motioned for Omega to follow.

Stepping into the open air, Omega saw the village spilling out across the hillside before him. Whereas the trash around his ship had been little more than a gigantic midden heap, he wanted to describe the garbage here as cultivated. Doors and windows appeared in haphazard intervals among the piles, the mounds themselves shaped into sunken bungalows. Between them, narrow streets and byways had been plowed into the scrap. These wound throughout the town the way a vine crawls between the bricks of a building.

It was the people that most caught his attention. Wrapped in rags the colour of their surroundings, these generational refugees moved about the piles with an assurance borne of long habit. Nearby, two villagers wrestled a wagon cobbled together from a storage container. Under a nearby canopy, three others sat laughing and passing a jug that might once have been part of an axle. A little ways off, a green child used a metal rod to shepherd a huge invertebrate creature through the streets. Despite the rickety look, the streets felt quite stable beneath his feet, though he found himself tripping occasionally on its uneven surface.

Ennis, noticing his difficulty, straightened his back somewhat and made the effort to take longer strides. He nodded to the men passing the jug as he went, and they barked a laugh. Omega could feel his guide's ridicule even if he couldn't hear it. Hoonra glided across the street as she did everywhere she went. He couldn't help noticing that nobody laughed at her.

"How many of you are there?"

"Less than before but, as I said, generations. We have built lives here despite the limits to our technology."

"And you expect to fit everyone onboard my ship?"

"No. Only the truly Faithful will be leaving. The others accept this."

The trio were approaching a low wall with a gate. Ennis nodded to the porter on duty before walking through. The landscape on the other side was a stretch of trash, beyond which the scrap seemed to be piled into columns, forming a sort of mockery of a forest. Ennis turned sharply and led the way to a pit a short distance off. He pointed for Omega to see.

The body at the bottom was fresh, the slash wounds across its face and chest clearly visible at a distance. Omega turned away quickly.

"You ought to warn people before you show them something like that!"

"There is a monster among us." Ennis' tone was grave but Omega shook his head, his laughter sardonic.

"No kidding? You mean to tell me there are dangerous critters lurking around a planet covered in garbage?"

"Critters? No. Not out beyond the wall. From within it. One of the Faithful has fallen. We moved the body here to stop the spread of panic from getting worse."

Hoonra had not turned away when Omega had. Instead, she had leaned down for a better look. "The cuts are deep and aggressive, but they are not wild, Omega. They were purposeful. Monsters aside, this attack was calculated."

Ennis nodded. "We do not have the weapons here to kill in this manner. This was done by a claw. One from the congregation has changed. I fear it is after the Dreamer. Kill it. Kill it and take us from here, and you can have your ship and the repairs besides."

Omega stood still for a minute, considering, before looking to Hoonra. The Lizardwoman returned his gaze for a moment, then gave a resigned shrug before looking back at the body.

"Yeah, I think we can do this," Omega said, "We'll need a few hours, and access to some of your salvage. Oh, and we want our stuff back, too. If you haven't done it already, put a watch on the Dreamer. Near sundown, call all of your Faithful together in front of the medlab. Tell them it's news about the ship, a miracle even, stir them up. Make them think they're leaving right away. We'll be ready."

Ω

Omega and Hoonra stood in the shade of an awning as, nearby, yet more of the mismatched villagers made their way from their ramshackle homes towards the yard in front of the medlab. The crowd had been gathering for half an hour now, and they were growing restless. Ennis stood with two guards by the door. He was clearly becoming uncomfortable with this many people packed so closely near the Dreamer.

Hoonra put her weight against the spear shaft she held, testing its strength. She checked the homemade beacon tethered to its end. "So, do you think this will be like chasing werebeetles on Arneil?"

"Maybe, but I was leaning more towards the week we spent with the warp-tigers on Chilldar."

"Ah yes." The Karackian nodded. "The tracker came in very handy then. Do you think this will give us that much chase?"

"Only one way to find out." Omega adjusted his belt and checked the settings on his helmet. "Come on. I think the crowd has stewed long enough. If there really is a fallen pilgrim among the crowd, they'll make their move anytime, or they'll miss their chance."

The pair of them approached, skirting the shuffling crowd to stand beside Ennis.

"It's about time." The Avatar was sounding even grumpier than before. "We all are ready." Ennis raised his voice and the crowd began to hush, "and you wanted an audience, did you not? To reveal to the Faithful news of the early departure."

Omega opened his mouth to speak but a sharp clang from within the medlab interrupted him. "That was even faster than I expected. One side, please, gentlemen, and follow me. Hoonra, get ready."

Omega and Hoonra stepped inside, followed closely by Ennis, the guards, and any other peasants brave enough to look.

One of the windowpanes was missing, but the Dreamer's tank stood at the back of the lab as it had before. Beside it, metal club in hand, stood a peasant who turned at their unexpected intrusion.

"Just who do you think you are?" Ennis shouted.

Omega turned to Hoonra. "You're right, this is a lot like the werebeetles."

The stranger stood stock still for a moment. Then, as Ennis motioned for the two door guards to move in, the peasant brandished the cudgel. "Entropy take you!" he yelled, slamming the club down on the Dreamer's tank. There was a sharp crack, and Ennis screamed.

"Now, Hoonra!" Omega motioned, but Hoonra was already moving. The great muscles in her legs propelled her across the room. With a mighty heave, she thrust her spear right into the peasant's chest. The man tried to scream but only a whining sound came out. He sank to his knees. The crowd stood in shock.

"Yeah, well done." Omega clapped slowly, turning to regard their slack-jawed faces. "Hoonra, ladies and gentlemen, the scourge of Karackas. Take a bow, Hoonra."

"I wish you would stop these theatrics, Omega. There is no honour in this kind of bragging."

"No, maybe not. But a job well done deserves recognition. You really walloped him."

Hoonra smiled a little at this. "Yes, I suppose I did. Its hide was thick and difficult to pierce."

"Look!" Ennis gasped.

Hoonra and Omega turned and could see the peasant clawing his way back to his feet. Omega felt a little impressed, though he could see that Hoonra was not.

As the peasant flexed its hand, his fingers elongated into the gigantic claws of a monster. It heaved its arm around, slashing through the medlab's wall and laying the room open to the night air. With one more great effort, the creature lifted itself up and, spear and all, tumbled out through the opening it had made.

"He'll get away!" babbled Ennis.

This time it was Hoonra's turn to become cross with the unpleasant man. "Your comments add nothing, Avatar. We can all see it escaping." Omega wasn't sure he'd ever heard her so annoyed.

They all piled back out the door. Outside, the crowd had dispersed upon seeing the monster ripping its way out of their hospital. The few stragglers that remained pointed off in the direction of the town gate.

"It's gone!" the Avatar cried. "It's gone, and it was a shifter. A shifter! We have been here for centuries; how could a creature of Entropy, a servant of the old Lords..." He trailed off as Hoonra's impressive bulk overshadowed him.

Omega stood beside her. "This'll be hard enough without stirring everyone into a religious frenzy. Keep calm. Hoonra, did you get the tracker good and stuck in its hide?"

The Karackian nodded, her stormy gaze never leaving the Avatar. "Good. Then we're off. Either we'll be back at sunrise, or *it* will."

That had been an hour ago. Now, Omega and Hoonra stalked their prey, moving quietly through the mounds of scrap metal beyond the gate. The moons cast strange and shifting shadows, forcing Omega to activate his helmet's night vision display. Luckily, Hoonra had tagged the creature pretty hard, pinning a makeshift tracker to it and injuring it in the process. They would catch up with it shortly.

Omega sidled up to one of the larger piles and watched as Hoonra ghosted past him. Her movements were smooth, assured. Once again, Omega marvelled at her utter silence, following her as she made for a nearby garbage column. Just as he reached her, there was a tremendous crash, and a groaning scream split the night.

Hoonra nodded. "It is badly wounded." Even in the inky dark, Omega could see the flush running through Hoonra's scales.

"Yeah, I heard it. That last crash was a bit theatrical, though. Don't you think it might be leading us on?"

"Leading us?" Hoonra sounded taken aback. "Were you not in the medlab?"

"Yes, Hoonra, I was certainly in the medlab."

"Then you saw me hit it. You saw the wound. To use your expression, I 'walloped' it. No, it is prey running for its life. It is for us to finish the job." Before he could say anything, Hoonra turned and slipped away. Omega followed.

The shuffling sounds which had led them were replaced by a heavy panting. Nearby, Hoonra crouched in the shadow of another cyclopean pile of debris, Omega peering over her shoulder.

The creature was motionless, hunched over and holding itself, the area around it somewhat more spacious than the rest of the rubbish-strewn landscape. Hoonra pointed to the long metal shaft that was stuck fully through its torso.

"Walloped," she whispered back to him.

"Yeah, fair enough." Omega leveled his ray-gun over her shoulder. "Like you said, time to finish the job."

"Wait, no," whispered Hoonra.

"Seems like a bad time to stop."

"Let me." Hoonra stood, shrugging Omega off with her customary grace. "It was a worthy foe, and an accomplished hunter in its own right. Honour demands, Omega."

"Best not to. Your blood's running pretty hot right now, Hoonra."

"My people are cold-blooded." Hoonra began backing away from him, keeping herself between Omega and the thing.

"You know damn well that's not what I meant," Omega hissed. "Now get out of the way. What good are bodyguards that don't do what they're told?"

Hoonra skipped back a few more steps, then turned, raising her sword above her head as she closed in. Omega craned his neck, but the creature seemed oblivious to her. He cursed and began circling the columns, trying to find a better vantage point.

Just as Hoonra took her last step, the shifter whirled, its heavy panting replaced by an animal scream. The creature tore the pole from its body. Spinning, swinging the pole like a club as it went, the monster caught Hoonra in the chest as her blade swung down, lifting her clear off the ground and launching her into a pile of refuse. Omega's jaw dropped.

"Hoonra!"

The thing turned to him as he yelled. It took a few hobbled steps towards him, throwing the spear haphazardly as it did so. Apparently not all of its injuries were feigned. The monster's features shifted then, the peasant's face melting into something longer and more sinister. Its legs and spine stretched, its fingers elongating further into huge carving-knife claws. It screamed again as it charged, breaking Omega's shock. He fired, his shaking hand sending the bolts wild.

The creature leapt and was nearly atop him when the ray-gun hit it. The blast landed somewhere on its upper body, sending it spinning. Omega felt the claws flash past his face before the bulk of the creature's shoulder bowled him over.

His headset worked to recalibrate itself after the impact, but Omega was still up before the shifter. He could see the thing dragging itself to its feet only a few meters away. When his display came back online, Omega saw that the creature's vital signs were fluctuating heavily. It turned, dazed. In its chest, just below the shoulder, a dark hole smoked. Something black oozed from the edge.

The creature shook its head and focused on Omega. It wasn't until it took another halting step forward that he realized he'd dropped his gun. He drew his pulsword from his hip as the shifter took another step. Things were not turning out the way he'd hoped. As the creature swung for him once more, he ran into the maze of rusted pillars.

Omega moved as quickly as he dared, trying in equal measures to stay both quiet and unseen. He was just about to take new cover when he saw it again. Ahead of him, a few meters to the left, one of the columns flexed a claw it shouldn't own. As his headset latched on to the silhouette, it outlined the shape of the thing, changed yet again. Now its body had become blocky, its arms and legs sprouting irregular growths and protrusions. It stood hunched over, its arms hanging to the ground like fallen struts, the claws splayed like old wire. It was facing away from him, waiting, obviously, for him to walk by.

Omega stayed totally motionless for a moment, but the creature didn't move. He hefted his pulsword, raising his arm into a striking position, biting his tongue at the sound of his flight suit moving. Still the creature remained frozen. Slowly, almost painfully, Omega took a step forward. The sound of his foot falling onto the rusted steel surface of the planet sounded like a landslide in his ears. By some miracle, though, the creature remained still. He took another step. Another.

Omega picked up speed, his footsteps as quiet as he could make them. He remembered the resistance Hoonra said she'd encountered when she'd stabbed the thing with her spear. He would need to put all his weight behind this strike if it was going to work. Before his eyes, his headset outlined a nerve cluster below the surface of the creature's skin. He tensed and moved in.

To Omega's credit, it did actually occur to him that he was being fooled in exactly the same way Hoonra had been. Just as he realized that Hoonra had been about the same distance from the creature when it attacked *her*, the thing spun around, long talons raking outwards. Instead of disemboweling him, the monster's whole paw caught him. Omega found himself airborne, crashing into a column of garbage much as the Karackian had.

This time it took Omega's headset more than just a minute to turn back on. When it did, it treated him to a close-up view of the creature's face as it hefted him from the wreckage, and raised him towards its open jaws.

Despite everything it had been through, the shapeshifter still possessed the strength to haul Omega into the air. He dangled above it, feet kicking feebly as he stared down into a mouth full of teeth, which he could swear were getting bigger as he hung there.

He could feel its claws digging into his shoulders, could feel the hot stink of its breath washing over his face. It was still panting, but now Omega could detect another sound beneath the heavy breaths. It was a kind of deep growl, like the engine of a freight car as it came barreling towards the listener. A sound made deep in the back of shifter's throat.

No. Not the shifter's throat. As Omega dangled within centimeters of his death, he found that he couldn't help but smile. "You know, she's normally dead quiet. You must have really ticked her off, big guy."

Hoonra's tackle came with the force of a hurricane, and once again Omega found himself flying. The trip wasn't as rough this time and, when he could orient himself, Omega saw where the real force had been directed.

Hoonra had knocked the shifter several meters across the junk yard. As it stood, she was already circling in again.

In all the time that Omega would know her, what he saw next would never leave his mind:

Hoonra moved with a fluid grace that Omega had not yet seen. She exuded focus and controlled malice. Her sword weaved in the air before her, her tail lashing back and forth in anticipation. The creature seemed confused by her display.

Calmly, she reached out a hand, beckoning the shifter to her.

The thing screeched and charged, the last reserves of its energy spent in propelling itself with sudden and incredible speed. It bore down on Hoonra, who stood now totally still, blade akimbo, waiting.

It seemed to Omega that the creature had already impacted Hoonra when he saw her move—or rather, caught up with the knowledge that she had done so. In one instant, she had been a statue in the monster's claws. In the next, she seemed to have slid fully through it, moving past its flashing talons like a dance tutor sidestepping her clumsy pupil.

She rounded, swinging her blade as she did so, slicing the beast's arm from its body at the shoulder. The cut was so clean that the monster didn't even lose speed. As it thundered past, Hoonra stepped into her own momentum and followed with a full-bodied, overhead arc. Her blade caught the creature at the crown of its head, tearing it like neatly creased paper. The force of the blow was so intense that the sword ground into the waste beneath, leaving Hoonra to pull it out.

Finally, she stood over the halved corpse, looking down, breathing heavily and leaning on her weapon. Omega took a tentative step forward, and Hoonra's head snapped up as if she'd forgotten him.

"Hoonra?"

She stared for a second longer, coming back to herself before she spoke. Finally, she nodded. "Walloped," she said, catching her breath.

"Yeah," replied Omega. "Walloped."

Ω

When the sun rose, Omega and Hoonra walked back through the village gates. Between them, trussed up in old wire, they dragged what little Hoonra had left of the shifter.

Omega turned to her. "You know, you talk a lot about honour and fair combat. Seems to me like tackling your enemy sidelong without any warning is pretty dishonourable."

"It had warning. I was not silent. Besides, much of my honour rests in keeping you safe. I doubt it would have dropped you had I taken the time to ask. I am, after all, your bodyguard."

"Sure, well, thanks for remembering. Joking aside, thanks as well for finding my sidearm." He patted the ray-gun on his hip. "It's sort of funny, don't you think, that it spoke to us in the medlab? I mean, not once all night did it say anything else."

"Were you hoping for some witty banter?"

Omega rolled his eyes. "Might have been more fun than this conversation has turned out to be. Seriously though, it is odd, isn't it? Bringing up old legends?"

"I suppose. It is not uncommon for prey to say any number of odd things while under the pressure of the hunt." Hoonra stopped, reading his body language. "Something is bothering you."

"Yes, I guess it is. It's just, I've never seen anything like it before. All that stuff it could do with its body. And to call Entropy down on us before trying to tear us limb from limb…"

"You act as though it were some sort of Void-walker. I didn't know you had any religious superstitions, Omega."

"You know I don't. Still…" Omega removed his helmet and scratched his head, but the words he sought weren't there. "I don't know how to describe it. Just gave me the creeps, I suppose."

"Karackians don't have 'creeps'."

Omega laughed. "Well, they had *one*, but I took her along with me. Come on. The locals are waking up." Omega and Hoonra hefted their load once more, turning past curious onlookers to return their catch to Ennis at the village square.

Ω

In the end, the repairs didn't take nearly as long as Omega had feared. Despite his unlikeable nature, Ennis had been right about the villagers' capabilities. Within a week and a half, the many hands of the town came together. The parts they used were old, seemingly archaic in some cases, and Omega was sure his ship would not pass any kind of formal health and safety inspection. That said, he was relatively sure the last iteration wouldn't have, either. After checking all of the major systems and most of the minor ones, Omega was prepared to declare the *Buccaneer II* ready for flight.

Leaving the atmosphere was tricky, but with the help of experience, and without the threat of imminent death to distract him, Omega navigated the storm cells in the upper atmosphere. Another week passed, and he and Hoonra were back in known space, docked at a major trade hub, happily waving good-bye to those villagers. They reported the existence of the Tellarian refugees as well, though they were unsure what the local governing Corporation might do about them.

For most of the trip, Ennis had ignored them. He seemed content to tend to the Dreamer and boss the other faithful around at his own discretion. In the end, he stood before Omega on the *Buccaneer's* ramp while the rest of the flock took care of their belongings. For just a moment, he seemed about to say something kind. Instead, he nodded, put back on his customary scowl, and moved down the ramp to harass the members of the congregation responsible for moving the Dreamer's tank.

Omega watched him go and shot Hoonra a sidelong glance. "You know, for a second there, I thought he was going to be civil."

"Don't be too hard on him." The voice that answered was decidedly not Hoonra's. "This Avatar is the most capable of my disciples, for now."

Omega found that the spaceport had gone suddenly quiet. Quiet and empty, save for a little girl with mismatched eyes standing beside him. He stepped back reflexively.

"It is incredibly unsettling when you do that. And I'm not one of your disciples. You got a free ride, and I got my ship back. End of story."

The girl gave a coy smile. "No, Omega. Not the end. Not by a long stretch. Remember your service to me, Omega Brown, when we meet again."

"If we ever meet again, the first thing I'll do is..." He stopped. The girl was gone; the spaceport was bustling.

Hoonra regarded him with a look that bordered on alarm. "You were doing it again."

"I told you, that kid can get inside your head."

"Not my head."

"No, of course not. Nothing to work with. Come on." He stepped back into the ship, keying the ramp closed as he did so. "It's time to find a new job."

Episode 3:
The Sorcerer of Space Station 9

The rush and swirl of hyperspace slid past the viewer, the mad electric-blue light bathing the cockpit. Omega checked the console controls once more. Nearly there.

"Hoonra," Omega called, as he keyed on the comm system to the gun turret, "tell me again why we're doing this."

"Because it is the right thing to do." The Karackian's sibilant baritone vibrated back through his headset. She sounded bored to be saying it again. "The people there will need our help. And because the governing Corporation managed to come up with a price that actually caught your attention. Their usual mercenaries will not take this job; regardless of our tab, they will remember the favour."

"I'm still not sure how useful an IOU from the Syndicate of United Systems will be. It's less a government and more of a...benevolent mafia."

"You are just worried about the Swarm."

"Well, aren't you? I mean, the reports about them claim they've beaten every organized fleet they've fought. Nobody understands the structures they build, or what they're after. The only fights they've withdrawn from are the ones they chose to leave."

"Technically, you could say that about nearly everyone."

"You know what I mean. Nobody understands those machines; where they strike or why. There's a reason the Corporate mercs don't want this job."

"Then it is lucky for the survivors on that station that we are more honorable than the mercenaries the Syndicate usually relies on."

Omega had just began to mentally question whether or not there would even be any survivors when the proximity alarm started flashing.

"Hope you're ready back there. Dropping out of hyperspace now."

As Omega moved the controls, the viewer filled suddenly with the immensity of a white-streaked, pink gas giant. The station in question was on the far side.

"No sign of any Swarm ships yet," Omega relayed. "Heading for cloud cover." The *Buccaneer II* brushed across the planet's atmosphere, pushing down until it could skim just below the upper layer of clouds.

This far up, the turbulence did little to rock the ship. Omega kept his eyes trained for any movement as the *Buccaneer* accelerated towards the space station in orbit.

It appeared over the horizon seconds later. At this distance, nothing appeared to be amiss. Omega checked his scanners, sucking his teeth. "I can't see anything out there."

"The Swarm has left?" Hoonra sounded hopeful.

"Not a chance."

The station drew closer, and Omega checked his scanners again. "Looks like some pretty precise work. Most of the structural integrity is intact, but I'm reading severe damage to a number of major systems." He rubbed his chin. "It's a bit weird, I can't get a clear picture of the wreckage. I wonder if—"

The *Buccaneer's* hailing system gave a choked, static cough, and then went quiet. Omega leaned in. "Hello?" he broadcasted. "Is there someone out there looking to say hi?"

There was silence again for a moment, then bursts of static and speech started coming through. Omega patched it to the internal comm.

"*Station 9* hailing... all systems... resistan... some kin... amming tool."

"What was that about?" Hoonra asked.

"You were right about survivors, I guess. Couldn't get much out of it, but I think he said something about a jamming tool."

Omega had barely finished speaking before laser fire began to batter the *Buccaneer's* hull. He cursed, accelerating as he rolled the ship. He checked his scanners once more. They showed nothing new.

"Where the hell are they?"

"I see them," Hoonra called back, "deep in the cloud cover. They are below us."

Omega corkscrewed upwards, leaving the clouds behind. His scanners still showed nothing, so he began cycling through the ship's external video feed. After a few flicks, he found what he was looking for.

A dozen or so arrow-shaped fighter craft had emerged from the pink haze. He could see Hoonra's lasers cutting out towards them, holding the squadron back. The *Buccaneer* had driven closer to the station, but the element of surprise had been lost. It was time to go.

As Omega reached for the hyperspace controls, the ship's hailer snapped back on. "This is *Station 9*. Can you hear us? You've made it closer than any other ship. Please respond."

Omega hesitated, his hand hovering above the console. Hoonra spoke before he could decide. "Aren't you going to respond?"

"I'd forgotten I was broadcasting that across the ship."

"Tell them we will be right there."

"Hoonra, we're about 20 seconds from being vaporized. We're done here."

"Omega…" He could hear the wound in Hoonra's voice. "We said we would help those people."

Before he could reply, the ship's speaker buzzed back to life.

"Attention unidentified ship. If you can hear us, head this way. No one else has made it off-system. The Swarm is—" The words cut out once more.

Omega ignored what Hoonra was saying now. He hurled the *Buccaneer* back around, surprising the Swarm squadron by driving directly into it. Hoonra shot one as they passed. As the ships dispersed, Omega turned again and flew straight for the station. The fighters regrouped quickly and resumed their pursuit but, as the *Buccaneer* approached Station 9, they broke off, returning to the anonymity of the cloudy giant. Omega leaned back in his chair, expelling his breath.

The station spread out before them, and he could see a likely hangar close by. He hailed them once more. "Thanks for the quick thinking there, *Station 9*. I'm heading in for a landing at the bay nearest my position right now."

"Negative," the signal from the station was much clearer now, "it's one of our occupied sectors. The Swarm controls various parts of this station. What are your intentions here?"

"Well, believe it or not, we're the rescue team." There was a moment of silence on the hailer.

"You'd better come inside then," the voice sounded tired, "sending the coordinates now."

Ω

Omega had finished checking all of his gear and the power to his rocket boots, and was just tuning his helmet to a frequency the station could recognize when Hoonra joined him by the exit ramp. She responded to his greeting with a curt nod.

"Look" — Omega activated the hatch controls and started down the ramp — "there's no need for the cold shoulder. We made it inside, didn't we?"

"A happy accident." Hoonra's tone felt decidedly frosty.

Around them, the lights in the hangar flickered, struggling to keep the little space illuminated. There was barely room for anything bigger than the *Buccaneer*. The walls were scorched in several places, and Omega was sure he could smell the remains of an electrical fire. As they covered the short distance from the ship to the door, Omega activated his forearm display, scanning the station schematics he'd been provided.

"Hey, I was only thinking about our safety, okay? How are we going to keep ourselves paid and fed, and bouncing around the galaxy if we get eviscerated?"

A step behind him, Hoonra stopped. "If our life's focus revolves solely around spending and eating," she began as he turned to face her, "then we are as good as destroyed already. You nearly turned us back on our word, Omega. It would have sacrificed our honour."

"This again, Hoonra? What good is honour if you're too dead to appreciate it?"

"Better to die with honour than live as a beast." She crossed her arms.

"Is that what I am to you?"

"No, Omega" — Hoonra's voice was deep and gentle — "you are my employer and my good friend. I had hoped, at this point, that I would no longer need to explain to you why doing something for the benefit of another is more than just a job." Before Omega could say anything, Hoonra asked, "Do you know where the survivors are hiding?"

"Yeah," he replied, his neck suddenly flushed. "Yeah, they aren't far." Without looking at his bodyguard, he projected the map he'd been considering into the space between them. "We're here, yes? If we follow the corridor outside and over, past these next two intersections we'll find them here. First door on the right.

"Two problems. First, Swarm bots control parts of the station and, judging from the ambush we experienced earlier, I'm sure they've set up patrols. No easy way for us to get the survivors past them as a group. Second, even if we get everyone back here, we still can't get off-system."

Omega deactivated the display. He found he still couldn't meet Hoonra's eyes. "I'm beginning to think the Swarm only let us land because they're sure their work here is inevitable. Whatever it is. They'll blow the whole thing away when they have what they want."

"Agreed, but there is no point in worrying about that yet." Hoonra hefted her sword. "The first problem we can handle. You go to the survivors while I create a distraction."

"Not a chance. Hoonra, I know you're good, but taking on the Swarm alone without anything other than a sword is suicide; I didn't even take mine off the ship."

"My weapon is of little import. I am a warrior; I will defeat them with whatever I can use, as honour allows."

"No." Omega looked directly at her. "You don't carry the equipment or firepower. I won't let...I mean, you aren't getting killed over this to prove..." The words caught in his throat, and he cleared it. "You find the survivors. I'll distract the Swarm." He started backing towards the door before she could respond. "Keep your communicator on channel 2, and stay low until you reach them. Once the fireworks start, we're going to have to move pretty quickly."

"You do not need to do this, Omega."

Omega shrugged and drew his ray-gun. When the hangar door slid open, he pressed himself against the jamb, peering into the hallway to make sure it was clear.

"Yes," he said to himself, "I do."

There were no less than three Swarm bots working around the huge set of heavy doors Omega found. He was impressed; he hadn't thought there would be anything the Syndicate could build that would slow those things down. The station's defences certainly hadn't. Carefully, he slipped around the hallway corner, drawing closer to the bots. It wouldn't be enough to just get their attention. Omega needed them to follow.

He took light steps towards them, jogging down the egg-white hallway to the juncture before ducking around the next corner. He'd seen other bots spread throughout the grid work of the halls, but all of them had seemed focused on a patrol pathway that led to this place. Whatever the Swarm wanted, it must be in that vault.

Provided that he stayed quiet and kept his distance, the bots had either not noticed him, or simply didn't consider him a threat. After his performance in orbit, he found he couldn't really blame them.

Omega looked at the ray-gun in his hand and considered briefly if he ought to try initiating things with one of his trademark, smart-mouthed quips. Instead, he turned back into the hallway, levelled the weapon and fired. The ray-gun's whining beam ripped out, catching one of the bots square in its back. It screamed, its voice grating and metallic, its tripod legs scrambling to try and turn the column of its torso towards the attack.

Omega fired again, severing one of those legs as the creature came around, its body toppling over, damaged, but clearly not fully dismantled. The bots on either side, meanwhile, had pivoted their bodies above the legs without hindrance. Omega ducked back behind the corner as their cutting beams lanced out, slicing and charring the wall where he had been.

Omega squatted down and rolled out past the edge. He fired again, this time catching one the bots that now faced him. His weapon melted an agonizing-looking hole through the bot, causing it to stagger, but it fired again, and Omega was obliged to roll back. He was beginning to see how these things had gained their reputation.

"Hoonra," Omega barked into his wrist comm, "things are getting plenty lively on this end. I'm going to start back to the ship."

"Noted. I will make my way to the survivors now." Omega keyed off the comm and edged his way back to the corner for a look at his targets.

He didn't have far to search. His conversation had only lasted a few seconds, but in that time the uninjured bot and its now stumbling partner had moved in on him. As he turned the corner, Omega was gripped by the wrist and jacket, hauled bodily from the floor by vise-like robot appendages. He yelled, kicking as the bot positioned him in front of its cutting laser.

Omega shot first, wildly, his beam tearing through the cutting laser and one of the robot arms. He was dangling suddenly from the bot's other appendage and his next shot went wide, catching the already injured bot in its torso, the beam scraping upwards into the red lens of an eye. The bot let out another of those awful grinding cries before toppling over.

Omega's elation at its defeat was erased by sudden pain. The bot that held him had electrified its arm, shocking him as he dangled. Omega's headset began to stutter, and he felt himself start swinging outwards as the bot swiveled its body. After a few turns it let go, and Omega sailed across the hallway intersection to crash fully against the far wall. He slumped to the floor, unmoving.

The bot followed after him, like an organic predator toying with its prey. It extended one of its lower arms, pulling Omega upright. It didn't occur to him until much later that this bit of luck had saved his life. Disoriented and semiconscious, Omega fired with his now freed hand. The beam sliced upwards, hitting the bot near its base, churning through its body and most of its circuitry. This bot made no sound as it died, instead slumping forward to rest against the wall above Omega as its systems gave out.

Omega lay there bewildered for a few seconds before he clambered out from underneath the mechanical corpse. His headset was still flickering, but he didn't need its display to hear fresh bots scuttling down the corridors in his direction. With a quick glance at the vault door for orientation, Omega worked his feet, stumbling down the hallway and back to the ship.

Ω

After Omega's call, Hoonra moved immediately. Recalling the map Omega had shown her, she went with speed and silence down the hallway. Further on, two bots rounded a corner, but they were moving in the opposite direction, regarding Hoonra not a bit. Still, the Karackian crouched at the hallway corner, peering around its edge before moving forward. From what she could recall, the survivors' room should now lie just a little way ahead.

Hoonra counted the doors as she passed, stopping where she thought appropriate. The portal before her looked just like all the

63

others; without Omega's map, she couldn't know for sure. Hoonra considered this situation for a moment. Then, she knocked.

The door swished open. Hoonra was greeted not by armaments and military equipment but by long white coats and diagnostic machines. The human man immediately across from her motioned for her to step inside. As the door shut behind her, Hoonra took in the rest of the room.

"You are the survivors we spoke to?" she asked.

"Yes," the man replied, "I'm Kirin. And you are one of the mercenaries the Syndicate sent to help us?"

"Warriors," Hoonra corrected, her gaze falling now on the balding man she was speaking with. "How did you know who I was?"

As if the answer was obvious, Kirin motioned to the equipment and survivors around him. "We could see you through the hallway surveillance screens. Also, the bots don't tend to knock. The Swarm has kept us corralled in here. It's a control room, but I don't think they care." Hoonra could hear the resignation behind his words. "Why should they? Nothing our mercs did even seemed to slow them down."

"Your mercs? Are you not warriors yourselves?"

"No, goodness no." Kirin turned from her, shuffling between the consoles and computing stations to stand beside one of the primary screens. Hoonra followed. "We're scientists. This station was meant for research; that's why it was overrun so easily." He frowned. "That said, I don't think that a full squadron of guards would have made much difference."

"What are you researching here?" Hoonra asked.

"Oh, the planet, of course. The clouds cover an incredible ecosystem, and the planet itself showed signs of having been inhabited by quite an advanced alien race. We managed to send a few expeditions down there, to what looked like an old tomb or religious site of some kind. It was just after we brought some of the relics back here that the Swarm showed up."

"Interesting. I hope for your sake that you found everything you had hoped for." Hoonra began walking back towards the door. "Now, though, it is time for us to leave." As she spoke, a number of scientists glanced up from what they were doing. All of them considered Kirin who, in turn, seemed to deflate even further.

"We can't go yet."

"Yes, we can." Hoonra did not stop moving. "Now."

"It's just," Kirin looked to his peers for aid, but as a group they seemed suddenly interested in their screens, "we can't leave the relics here. Really. They're one of a kind artifacts. And the Swarm wants them, for some reason, which means they must be something special. We just haven't had a chance to give them a thorough examination yet." Before Hoonra could answer, Kirin motioned for her to join him at the nearest console. In it, she could see the burned remains of three different bots all scattered around a very impressive set of doors. "We've been watching that friend of yours," Kirin continued. "He's pretty handy with that firearm, but it won't last. What you see there is the vault door. It seems to be the only thing we've got that the Swarm hasn't simply sliced through. The relics are inside. Look, there's more than enough of us to carry what we need out of there, and we can be quick. That door is just a block or so away. Help us get what we need from there, and then you can take us out of here."

"Unacceptable." Hoonra's answer was so sharp that Kirin winced.

"Well," he began, "then we aren't going with you. You can just leave us here. We've figured out a way to blow the station." As he spoke, a few of the other scientists looked over their shoulders. Hoonra could see that none of them were enthusiastic. "We've all talked. We've put too much time into this for the Swarm to make off with it now. They think we're not a threat, but they haven't been paying enough attention to us here." He straightened his back. "If you won't help us, you might as well leave. We'll start the sequence once you're off."

Hoonra stood there for a moment, regarding the much smaller man before her. She could see the sweat droplets forming on his head. Finally, she spoke. "You defend your work out of honour? You would rather die than see it destroyed or undone?"

"Yes," Kirin managed. Hoonra nodded.

"I understand. We will retrieve your relics. Omega has provided the distraction. And we will be quick. He needs us." Hoonra scanned the screens. She could see Omega now, moving down another hallway. He was taking the long way back to the ship, buying her all the time she would need to get the scientists away. Behind him, laser blasts flashed, marring the walls as he dodged passed. She raised her communicator.

"Omega," she called. The communicator spat static back at her. She frowned and motioned to the controls. "I need to speak to him through your device."

"Can't. The Swarm shut those down shortly after you got here. I think they figured we were up to something when you chose to land. They're self-assured but not totally oblivious."

"Then we must be quick," said Hoonra, marching back to the door, "More than quick. We go for your relics. Be ready." She opened the door before Kirin could answer, urging the now-scrambling scientists into the hallway with her.

Ω

Omega had decided that the next time, regardless of equipment or feelings of guilt, it would be Hoonra's turn to be the bait. He dropped to one knee as he heard another bot approaching. When it rounded the nearest corner, he fired, catching its front leg and severing it. The machine toppled forward and, as it did, Omega fired again, boring a hole through the top of its cylindrical head.

He shifted to a crouch, anticipating the other two bots in the triad. As he stood, he fired a quick burst of his rocket boots, propelling him through the air and past the corridor entrance. His weapon cut a continuous beam as he leapt, slashing the next bot from one side to the other, darkening its single red lens.

Two of three down, but he nearly fell instead of landing when he saw another eight moving in. He hit the ground running while electricity and laser blasts charred the wall behind him. That trick had worked not one corridor back. The bots, it seemed, were becoming annoyed. They weren't too fast, which was lucky for him, but they were tough. And well-armed. And, increasingly, they were everywhere.

Omega had begun by the vault door and taken off in what he assumed was the direction of the hanger. This turned out not to be the case. Between the monotone grid of the station's white and chrome corridors, and the probable concussion given to him earlier, Omega had gotten himself turned around—and more and more trapped. The distraction, he decided, had gone on long enough. Omega fired under his arm at the horde that would now be rounding the corner, and then keyed his wrist comm.

There was no response.

Cursing, Omega pressed himself into a door jamb, the thin ledge providing scant cover. He tried his comm again, keying the maps as he did so.

Again, no response. Omega remembered the electrical charge that had shot up his arm. He spit.

"Why do these things never go the way I envision?"

He crouched and used his rocket boots to hurl himself into motion once more, but the bots had learned his technique. Their shots didn't hit him properly, but they did overload the lighting panel above him. Omega crashed to the floor, his boots forcing him further onwards and into the next intersection. Lasers scorched the floor behind. He reached out, yelling as he went, catching a panel edge of the hallway corner as he zipped passed. He hung on, using his momentum to swing around the corner and slide to the left down this new passage.

There were bots here as well, but only a triad and, though they fired, their shots were erratic, surprised by Omega's impromptu strategy. Omega, meanwhile, tried his utmost to make the best of this literal turn of events. He brought his ray-gun around, splashing the hallway with sustained beams. He scorched the lead bot, but his high speed slide prevented any kind of accuracy. The bots, finally, began strafing the floor, blocking the hall as they did it.

Shooting again, and laughing at the break-neck stupidity of it all, Omega decided to double down. He pushed himself off the floor with his hands and tucked in his legs as best he could, launching himself upwards, level with their heads. He fired again, drilling one bot above the lens before flicking his arm, melting a deep gash across the other's head and torso. This manoeuvre unbalanced his flight, twirling Omega directly into the third bot. He had just enough presence of mind to deactivate his boots before impact.

The pair of them tumbled backwards, rolling over each other and into the wall behind. Having seen the hit coming, Omega pulled himself upright first. As the bot began righting itself, he fired. The bot hadn't yet stood again before he'd put it back down.

Omega winced a little as he rose, rubbing his shoulder. "I wonder if the guards here tried any of that." Behind him, at the other end of the hallway, the bot horde had finally caught up. Omega ducked their first volley and looked around. For once the hallways ahead of him seemed clear. Trusting his luck, and with little other choice, he jogged towards the most likely route. It was time to get back to the ship.

Ω

Hoonra had managed to herd the scientists along at a fair pace, and without any interference from the Swarm. Wherever Omega had gotten to, he'd certainly provided an appropriate distraction. As the team neared the vault door, Kirin emerged from the pack.

"I have the key card," he said, producing it from one of his many pockets. "I just need to check something first."

"I am sure you can check once the door is open." Hoonra stood with her back to the vault, scanning the halls.

"No, it's not like that." Kirin leaned close to a tiny readout screen, punching keys as he did so. "This isn't just a safe. It's a decompression chamber. The surface pressure on that gas giant is extraordinary. We couldn't just bring the artifacts out without trying to stabilize them; they'd have exploded. We were waiting for the decompression experiment to finish when the Swarm showed up."

Hoonra glanced over her shoulder. "Did you say experiment? As in, if the experiment fails, there will be nothing of use inside this chamber?"

"Uh" — Kirin bit his lip — "well, yes. What we were doing, it's never been tried before. Nobody's ever made it to the surface of that world before, let alone brought anything back with them. A major part of our work here was testing to see if it could even be done."

Hoonra turned fully, regarding the vault door. "And not a mark here from the Swarm."

"It's extraordinary, isn't it? Of all the things that stopped them, I can't believe this door was the exception."

Hoonra shook her head. "It did not stop them. You say they arrived just after the experiment started? They knew. This is why they kept you alive. They wanted you to do the work for them." The scientists huddled together by the door looked at each other in disbelief.

"They weren't trying to get inside." Kirin's face reddened as the realization hit home. "They were monitoring the test. They were guarding it."

"Is it complete?" Hoonra asked. Kirin looked back at the onscreen readouts.

"Yes, just a few minutes ago, in fact." He frowned, rubbing his chin. "These readouts are not what I expected. The test is complete, and the sensors say that there is something inside but..." He looked to his colleagues and then back to Hoonra. "Well, only one way to know for sure, right?" Kirin keyed the door control.

There was a rumbling sound in the walls as the pressure locks gave way. The door sank into the floor.

The lighting inside was obscured by cloud-like vapours floating around, and Hoonra could see very little. Kirin stepped in, his peers behind him, and began wading through the dispersing fog. Someone moaned.

"What is it?" Kirin asked, and then he too let out a small wail. "No, no!" He lifted the remains of a vase from the floor. Holes spread across its surface, and it cracked a little as he held it. "It didn't work. Not properly anyway. Dammit." He looked around. "There must be something worth salvaging in here." He motioned to the other scientists. "Have a look, everyone. We have the data records at least, but there must be something physical worth taking with us."

Hoonra looked back, scanning the halls once more before moving in. The fog at the front of the chamber had mostly dispersed, revealing what looked like a large stone box. Cracks had formed along its sides, and the lid was partially disintegrated.

"What is that?" she asked.

"We weren't sure. A sarcophagus of some kind, we assumed." Kirin stepped forward and peered in. "Looks like it's empty."

"Yes," Hoonra agreed, looking past him through the lessening fog, "it is now."

Kirin looked up, puzzled. "What do you mean, now?"

Hoonra said nothing, pointing behind him instead. Kirin turned.

"Gods of Harmony," he gasped.

"No," said Hoonra, as the hooded figure at the casket's end stepped forward, "I do not think Harmony has anything to do with this."

Ω

Over the years, Omega had learned that it was important to count personal victories whenever they came, even the little ones. For example, he considered it a victory that he had, by some miracle of chance, managed to navigate himself back to the portion of the station where he'd parked his ship. The fact that the process of doing so had seemingly attracted the attention of what must be *absolutely every bot available* had not diminished this victory for him. It wouldn't either, provided that he managed to board the *Buccaneer* without becoming riddled with laser holes.

Any pretense of art or grace that Omega had put into his diversion was gone. His escape had become pell-mell. He dove from alcove to door jamb to hallway corner, all the while firing backwards, hoping to hit anything. Taking the time to aim had become far too dangerous, and it occurred to Omega that his only real advantage now came from the fact that there were simply too many bots behind him for them all to manoeuvre and shoot with any precision. Another little victory.

Omega rounded the last corner and bolted, his eye on the hangar door. He could hear the bots closing behind him, but it didn't matter any longer. Getting inside the hangar would allow him to lock the door. Hoonra was likely already aboard, engines primed, waiting for him to arrive. He just needed to get there.

He banged against the door controls, jabbing at them distractedly while looking back down the hall. He fired at the first red lens to round the corner. It felt like ages for his fingers to find the overly large door control. He fired again, but there were too many targets now for it to matter. He flattened himself against the door and shot again, his fingers finally landing on the right spot.

The hangar door slid open and Omega fell in. He scrambled to his knees, slamming the switch that closed the door and locked it. He slumped then, his forehead pressed against the steel control plate, his chest heaving. Just a moment. Just a second or two to catch his breath. But when he finally stood and turned, it was knocked back out of him again.

Hoonra was not aboard the ship, nor were she or any of the survivors in the hangar. Instead, Omega turned to find himself confronted by over a dozen bots. All of them had their weapons trained on him, yet for some reason, they weren't firing. Omega leaned back against the wall, shaking his head.

"What, do you all have some collective flair for the dramatic? Shoot, already."

There was a faint crash from the hallway—something electrical discharging—but Omega didn't care. The bots remained motionless.

"I hope Hoonra makes it out," Omega breathed. Then, louder: "Are you all on standby or something? I haven't got all day here."

He glanced over at the door, hearing another burst of electricity. This one sounded considerably louder than the last. "Just standing around while your friends cut their way in?" Omega hefted his ray-gun once more. "Y'know, I don't really feel like waiting around for the fight to start."

He drew a bead on the closest bot, wondering, briefly, how badly it would hurt when the others started torching him. Before he could find out, as a single body, the bots surged forward. Ignoring Omega, the bots seemed fixated on what was happening out in the hall. They didn't have long to find out.

The metal of the door changed rapidly from cold white, to seared black, to livid red and yellow, all within a second. The metal began to distend, then stretch, until finally it peeled inwards from the centre.

As the hole widened, lightning poured through the gap. The bots didn't even have a chance to start shooting. As a group they were lifted from the floor, the energy holding them aloft even as it tore and burned them.

They might have been screaming in that horrible grating voice of theirs, but Omega couldn't hear them. He was, in fact, only peripherally aware of them at all. As soon as the door had split open, Omega found his thoughts pulled inexorably to the figure pushing through the gap. The room seemed still to him now, almost silent. All he could be sure of was the sound of his own heartbeat, and the creature who now stood before him.

It was dressed in long, black robes, its face a mass of tentacles writhing beneath six ink-dark eyes. Golden embroidery flowed down its robes, forming symbols and letters that seemed to move and reform as Omega watched. The thing approached him now, its dark green arm extending to his temple while the other channelled the spray of lightning at the bots. It was painful to look at, and Omega dreaded its touch, but he couldn't move at all.

When its finger alighted, Omega's mind was filled with images he couldn't understand, conflicts raging across planets and star systems he'd never dreamed of before, tears in space and time where huge intelligences waited and watched. Beneath it all, a desperation, a certainty of failure before a task could be completed.

This creature was dying, he realized, and it was trying to tell him something before that happened. He saw the planet they orbited, saw the Swarm ships leaving the system, knew that they were afraid, even as the creature began to disengage. He noticed a sound then, a chant, repeating itself beneath the roil of his vision, a noise becoming concrete. One word. *Cirella.*

The hand on his head released him, but instead of freedom, Omega found himself compelled to raise his left arm. Vaguely, he was aware that Hoonra and the other survivors were in the background, that Hoonra wanted to help, and that she was just as powerless as he.

The creature took hold of his left hand. When the lightning brushed his skin, he thought the pain of it might drive him mad. It tore up his arm, his neck, across his bones. Omega felt as though his teeth might rocket out of his mouth as the energy shook him.

He had no idea how long the thing held him like that, power flying through his body, visions of a strange past saturating his mind. He became aware of time again only when he felt the creature withdraw, its presence dwindling. The thing's skin began to pale, its eyes withering, its tentacles spasming and then dropping, limp. It began to crumble before his eyes. In seconds, it was nothing more than dust and a pile of cloth and strange bones on the hangar floor.

It took time for Omega to become fully aware of his surroundings again. At some point, he realized he must have fallen to his knees, his hand still extended up to where the creature had held it. Around him, the floor was covered with the bodies of broken bots. He blinked, his voice returning:

"I beat you back to the ship."

Hoonra rushed forward, catching him before he could collapse. She settled him back against the hangar wall, crouching next to him. Beside her, one of the survivors stepped in.

"This is Kirin. He and the other scientists here discovered something on the planet they did not expect." It was always a little difficult for Omega to read her features, but he was sure that Hoonra looked frightened. "It was a sorcerer, Omega, a thing from the outer realms."

"What? What are you talking about?"

The man beside Hoonra stepped forward, motioning to Hoonra's arm. "Look what it did to her," he said.

"To you?" Omega asked.

"And to you. You saw the visions, yes. You heard the word?" Hoonra held up her left hand, dragging Omega's up as she did so. On both he saw matching symbols: the outline of a circle, like a child's depiction of a sun, split in two. His half was cut into the skin, jagged, erratic, the flesh bruised reddish purple. Hoonra's was measured and stable, straight raised lines pressed neatly into her scales.

Omega snatched his hand back, brushing the mark tenderly before looking to Hoonra. "What the hell have we gotten ourselves involved with?"

Episode 4: The Mark of Doom

Every night since Station 9, Omega saw the same thing in his dreams. There were planets on fire, whole star systems long torn apart by warring factions. There were intelligences behind this slaughter as well, a sense of great unknowable powers reaching for control over one another.

Above and behind it all, the name Cirella echoed, and Omega could see the face of the creature that he and Hoonra had freed, its ink dark eyes boring into him as the lightning it summoned etched symbols into his hand.

He would wake at this point, every time, shouting and sweating in his bunk on the *Buccaneer*. He hated that dream. The truth was, it scared him nearly to death.

Hoonra, meanwhile, had developed a decidedly different attitude to the whole thing. While the ordeal had affected them both, Hoonra had taken the encounter with the alien creature seriously, almost religiously so. She had been chosen for a higher purpose, she felt, whatever it was, and she was committed to it. Her honour demanded that.

Only, as Omega had pointed out at the time, her honour was already committed—to his service and he did not feel especially excited about the idea of being chosen. Hoonra hadn't spoken to him for days after he'd told her to forget about it. She'd only begun to open up again when he'd told her that he already knew what and where Cirella was, and reluctantly agreed to investigate.

This was how Omega now found himself riding in a makeshift boxcar on the edge of the city, travelling towards its foundations. Cirella had once been a vibrant metropolis, but that was ages ago. Now, it was mostly a mining planet. Hundreds of guilds and corporate entities had spent time retrofitting the ancient and alien architecture of Cirella's single, gigantic city into something their workers could use.

Networks of tunnels ran below Cirella's harsh surface, taking thousands of labourers into mines that stretched across the planet's northern hemisphere. The workers accessed these tunnels, which lay just outside Cirella City, via lifts which carried them from the upper levels down to the hardpan around the city's base.

Most of these lifts were large and in good repair, but Omega and Hoonra were not going where most workers would go. Instead, the contact they'd met had directed them to a spot in the city's actual foundations. These were truly ancient, an unknowable maze of web-worked girders and honeycombed concrete. It was a place for secrets, for things lost between the cracks. Nobody willingly went there, so it felt typically appropriate to Omega that he should have to.

Eventually the car shuddered to a halt. This particular sublevel was as far down as Omega and Hoonra could reach by mechanical transit, and it looked even more desolate than the level they'd just left. Even the shanty communities of the upper levels were gone. There was no attempt at creating permanence amidst the already existing structures here at all.

Omega looked at his wrist link. "It's hard to tell, but I think this is the place. Even if I'm wrong, this has got to be as far down as we can go without breaching the foundation."

"This seems incorrect. Why would they want us here?"

"Have I not been asking that for hours? I'm not wrong, Hoonra; this is the place. There's no one here."

"It is not what I expected." She couldn't hide her doubt.

"Look, we've gone the distance here, Hoonra. I know you wanted to see this vision thing through but—"

"There are scars, Omega, brands in our flesh. They cannot be ignored."

"And why not? The universe is full of nonsense that doesn't add up. Why should this? Look around you, Hoonra, and face the facts; there's nothing—"

The explosion ripped the words from his mouth. Omega was falling before he had any idea that something was wrong. Stonework and concrete buffeted him from every angle. After that he knew nothing at all.

Ω

The last clear view Hoonra had of Omega was the blast hurling him away. There had been a quick change in his expression, just a glimmer of understanding, and then everything had gone glaring white. She'd tried to call out, but was thrown from her feet, landing on her back a few meters away. Then, the world was made of dust, and a high-pitched ringing in her ears she could not shake.

"Omega!" She pushed herself upright as the tinnitus wore off. There was no response, and she called again. Silence.

As her pupils adjusted, Hoonra could see the collapse. A large section of the ceiling had fallen in, and the support beams beneath lay twisted and useless.

"Omega?"

81

He had been right there, right beside her, where now there was only a pile of slag. He'd told her there was nothing here, and now he wasn't there either. Hoonra began excavating the pile frantically, ripping up bits of rubble, scraping her fingers and forearms as she went.

How could she have been so stupid, so blind? Omega had warned her that the mark would not be worth pursuing, and now she knew he was right. Not only had she failed to discover its significance, but she'd failed in the duty she'd been hired for. Hoonra fell to her knees. With Omega dead, there was nowhere for her to go; her honour was lost. Hoonra curled forward, resting her head against the rubble. She would stay this way, she thought, stay and be the last monument to her own defeat.

She felt cold kneeling there, and was sure this must be the shame of her own death approaching. When she did not die, she guessed it might be something else.

Hoonra pressed her hands against some of the wider cracks below her. There was cool air coming through. She stood and attacked the ruined heap, hauling back fragments until she had removed enough from the edge to see the truth.

The concrete below her was thick, but incredibly old. The collapse had taken the roof certainly, but also some of the floor as well. There was a space in the level beneath her. She pressed her face to the widened crack.

"Omega?"

There was still no answer, but that didn't matter now. He would be there. After all the things that had nearly killed them, surely there was still some luck left.

Hoonra began to heft more stonework away, but halted abruptly. Something was approaching. The whir of tiny gears spinning, metallic feet clicking against the concrete floor. She wasn't sure what it was until she could make out the low buzzing that constituted their language. Swarm bots.

Hoonra ducked away from the heap. At least she had found the source of their trouble. The bots wanted something, something tied to the marks she and Omega had received during their last encounter with the machines. That must be it.

If they were here, then there had to be other ways down, other cracks she could find. She would rescue Omega, and together, they would find out what was going on.

Ω

Consciousness returned by degrees. At first, Omega was aware of dim discomfort—a feeling like a distant siren getting closer. Eventually, he noticed his headset beeping and opened his eyes to a blinking display. Static played across the readouts from inside his helmet, the images occasionally flickering out altogether. That gadget still worked, more or less, but the news it gave him was grim. His flight suit and body armour were heavily compromised.

In particular, his right shoulder was spectacularly broken. His emergency systems, or at least the ones that still functioned, were doing what they could to support and stabilize the area, but soon Omega would need much more than a field dressing and drugs.

The world outside his helmet was little better. It looked nothing like the last place he remembered; a landslide of concrete and metal lay around him, and the fleeting light he saw above filtered down

83

through cracks in the stone structure. The walls were close to him, and the fracture in the rock ripped downwards on one side. A collapse in the foundation seemed most likely. The ceiling extended well above him, and though it felt a little like a narrow mountain crevasse, it actually amounted to something like an access tunnel.

"Hoonra?" There was no answer. Was she down there with him, smashed beneath a pile of concrete? Omega's scanners could detect nothing beneath the rockslide. And of course they wouldn't, Omega thought, because Hoonra wasn't there. Of course she had avoided the worst of it. Of course it was his luck to be stuck, injured and alone. Their entire trip had been a waste; it was only natural it should end like this.

Omega extracted himself from the debris. If he ever ended up finding her again, he and Hoonra would be having a long talk about her contract and whether or not she might be better off staying with her own people on Karackas. Slowly, feeling his way and scanning with his helmet as he went, Omega moved further down the tunnel.

He wasn't sure how far he'd travelled by the time he saw light ahead of him. Twice in that place, he'd been sure he'd heard something flitting off in the dark above him, but his helmet had detected nothing. Closer up, he could see that it wasn't an exit at all, but more like a rockfall. The outer wall had tumbled away, as had much of the stonework beneath it. This section of the inner foundations was exposed to the Cirellan desert. Omega could already feel the heat and wind, but there was something else. A sound. He could hear laser fire.

Omega peered down the slope, then swore and stepped back. Below him, four Swarm bots had created a small outpost on top of the rubble left by the rockslide. As he watched, the tripod-like robots continued firing on a group of humanoids ascending the broken terrain. It took Omega a moment to place them. They were shifters, like the thing that had nearly killed him on Tellaria. They were changing themselves as they attacked, the foremost among them turning their bodies to angled shields as more piled in behind.

By the time they'd reached the bots, the vanguard had fallen, pushed aside by the ferocity of their kin. These now threw themselves upon the bots, drowning the noise of robotic weaponry beneath the violence of their own flesh. It was a massacre, bots and shifters alike tearing each other to pieces.

After a few moments, only one shifter remained. It took two or three stumbling steps past Omega's sight, and he realized the wall breach had exposed lower levels of the foundation as well. He could hear the shifter tumble, its injuries winning at last.

Swarm bots should *not* be in Syndicate space. That, and the fact that the last time Omega had seen them, he'd been given the mark on his hand, had to be more than a coincidence. Of course, none of that even began to suggest a reason for the shifters' presence. Omega needed to find Hoonra, but there was an opportunity here he couldn't pass up. He began picking his way down the slope.

Ω

Two more bots walked past Hoonra. After finding a chasm wide enough to pass deeper into the foundation, she had begun timing their movements. There were dozens down here, and it didn't take her long to realize they were performing a patrol. As the two beneath disappeared, she began to let herself down from the stone slab she'd climbed. This was the trick; trailing the bots close enough to hear and follow without revealing herself. Twice now she'd been nearly caught, and was still a little shocked to think that the machines had overlooked what must obviously have been her shoulder sticking out past a bent support post.

These bots seemed particularly talkative, and tracking was easy. It set Hoonra on edge. Something rankled about their single-mindedness which she couldn't place. Perhaps they had been this oblivious last time as well, but she wasn't convinced. They'd certainly been more deadly, but they'd also been expecting a fight. The things had an utterly alien intelligence; nobody really knew what controlled them. Hoonra didn't like her position hiding amongst them, but if she wanted to find Omega, she had no other choice.

Hoonra hadn't any idea what the tripod-shaped robots were discussing, but she heard when their voices started to echo. There was a chamber ahead, and Hoonra caught up with them just as the last one entered it. Creeping forward, she peered inside.

The place was cavernous. Bots, maybe twenty or thirty, milled about performing various excavation tasks. They were digging some kind of structure out from the rocks. The light from the hanging bulbs revealed an alien-looking latticework in the shape of a pyramid, intricately detailed ebony-coloured metalwork flowing together to form the topmost point. Tunnels led downwards into the structure, but Hoonra couldn't see what lay beyond them

There was movement from behind, the sound of metal prods scratching against stone. She hadn't forgotten her count; the bots had changed their schedule. Did they suspect her? Rather than waiting to find out, Hoonra looked for cover. There was nothing near her now, no way to hide in the entrance. She dashed forward. She could be silent when she wanted, or nearly so, but the sight of a sword-carrying Lizardwoman pelting through the cave was bound to be noticed quickly.

After three running strides, Hoonra threw herself behind a jutting ledge, lying flat. Rocks scraped together as she hit the ground, and she could immediately detect the bots warbling in louder tones.

It wouldn't be long now. Hoonra hadn't seen any enemies in the direction she'd run, but when she glanced back over the ledge, she saw that the bots behind her had fanned out. They'd detected something, and when they caught her, they'd pull her apart. Certainly, if those three couldn't manage it, their replacements would.

Hoonra reached out and snatched a stone. She threw it up in a wide arc, hoping she'd remembered the orientation of the chamber correctly. She didn't breathe again until she heard the stone clang against the metal structure before clattering down the far side.

The room buzzed immediately. Bots abandoned their jobs and rushed to investigate, even the ones who had been nearly upon her. The chaos was what she needed, but it wouldn't last. She looked back to the pyramid. Closer now, its patterns were more visible. From her vantage point, Hoonra could just see the outline of a symbol that looked strikingly like her scar. So, this was where they had taken Omega—or where they had planned to take him after the attack.

Hoonra sprang up and was down at the nearest entrance before any of the bots noticed. She pulled her sword from her back. The tunnel was tight for her size, and she would need to move quickly if this had any chance of working at all.

"I am coming, Omega," she whispered, and went in.

Ω

After he had clambered down the rubble pile as best he could, Omega found a smaller space behind it, a cave far beneath the city. At the back of this cave, a doorway and a section of decorative wall had been exposed. The entire structure was impossible to see, but he could make out black metal, which had been detailed and shaped into a doorway. It was covered in designs he didn't understand. It looked to Omega as if a building had been purposefully folded into the city's stonework, an elaborate but effective way to hide something that shouldn't be distributed.

No sooner had he entered than he was struck by a feeling of giddiness. Omega rushed into the darkness before he stopped, realizing what he was doing. His scar itched terribly. Something pulled at it, at him. He should not be here. Every ounce of his intuition told him he was in danger. His shoulder too, which had been useless during his scramble down the hill, was in much worse shape now, despite his trying to protect it. And above all of this, Omega was certain that if even Hoonra was still alright, there was almost no chance she would be somewhere ahead of him.

No way forward, no way back. Omega had lived the majority of his life weighing risk against reward. There had always been another option, but here he found none.

For the first time since his childhood, Omega felt utterly helpless. In the midst of this fear, one idea began to take hold: Hoonra shouldn't have forced them to help those scientists. If they'd just left the solar system like he wanted, none of this would have happened. And now she wasn't even here, hadn't even been able to spot the trap laid out for them. Some bodyguard. All that talk about honour and protection, and she was gone when he needed her most. Hoonra had gotten him into this, and he was going to have to do the work of fixing her mess. Cautiously, scanning with all of the sensors he had left, Omega moved further into darkness.

The hallway was not as long as it had seemed. Though the walls rebuffed all of his attempts at scanning, he could soon see faint light emanating from farther ahead. This came from a not-too-distant doorway which opened into a wide room with vaulted ceilings. Dim light suffused the air from an unknown source. Omega switched off his helmet.

It was a temple or reliquary of some kind. Omega could think of no other words to describe it. There were rows of stands equally distanced throughout the vast space. Many still held objects, but most had fallen into piles between the pillars. Towards the center of the room, Omega could see an obelisk made from the same faintly shining obsidian substance as the walls and pillars. The itch in Omega's hand started again.

The walls were not unadorned as he had initially thought. Instead, there were panels set into the stone; these seemed to be the source of the room's dim light. As he neared the panel closest to the door, the light grew a little brighter. It was a plaque, he could see, and it seemed to respond to his presence. He could make out some small images, which, as he looked more closely, began to move.

Ω

The inside of the pyramid was a maze. Matte black paneling covered the walls of the rooms and hallways, and strange light emanated from a source Hoonra couldn't identify. She had felt odd as she entered, sudden vertigo disorienting her as she walked through the entrance. When the moment passed, she could see no reason for it and wondered if she was being held somehow or scanned, but nothing else hindered her. The script she had seen carved into the outer walls continued throughout the whole structure. The symbols made no sense, but Hoonra felt they should, as if they were ready to tell her something if only she could see it. She dared not stop for a closer look.

Thus far, she'd met no resistance, a fact which troubled her. She'd expected the bots to be on her tail, if not already inside, yet she found herself walking through room after empty room, their purpose as alien as the script on the walls. They were filled with weird consoles and strange displays. Ultimately, Hoonra's only real sense of direction came from two things: first, from her scar, which had become steadily more irritated since she had entered, and second, from the descent itself. Hoonra felt very much that she was travelling down into the gut of something huge and sleeping. She was no longer sure if it would be Omega she found in its center.

At last, Hoonra passed through the doorway at the bottom of yet another ramp and stopped. The half-light was brighter here, green-tinged, the room bigger than she had thought possible at the center of this place. It formed a giant silo with doorways and catwalks all leading to a teardrop-shaped crystal chamber on a pillar in the middle. Hoonra could see there was something inside. Her scar ached. Steeling herself, she crossed.

The bottom of the chamber was open, the catwalks all meeting in a ring around its base. There was a seat there with restraints, but Hoonra thought it looked more like a throne. It was surrounded by more bizarre-looking machinery, all of which led up into a pod suspended above the seat. Despite how strange it seemed, Hoonra was sure she'd seen that pod before. The last time, she'd been told it was an incubator. "No," she whispered, "surely not."

"Yes, Hoonra, I'm afraid so, though I am glad to see you remember me."

Hoonra spun, sword raised. Behind her stood a human child. She was dressed plainly in a long white dress which fell nearly to her feet. She regarded Hoonra with a patronizing smile, and mismatched black and white eyes.

"How did you get here?" Hoonra kept her blade up as she spoke, sidestepping back towards the catwalk she'd come from.

"Oh, I belong here. This place was made for me. For us, actually."

Hoonra ignored the offered bait and asked, "Where is Omega?" She continued sidestepping, stopping when she felt herself brushing close to a pillar. She'd counted the pillars when she'd gained the platform. She hadn't lost track. There shouldn't be anything beside her.

"Is there something in your way, dear-heart?" The girl gave a look of feigned concern.

Hoonra glanced to the side and saw nothing. It was impossible; she'd felt an object with the side of her tail. Unnerved, she looked again.

The electrical blast that buckled her knee came out of nowhere. Hoonra cried out in shock, clutching her leg as she looked frantically for the source of the attack.

"Disoriented, Hoonra? This should help." The girl waved her hand as if brushing away smoke. Instantly, Hoonra felt that sense of vertigo again, her vision blurring. Sounds flooded her ears, but Hoonra felt they'd been there for some time, that she was just now noticing something she'd been hearing in the background all along. The whirring and winding of tiny gears. Metallic prods clacking against the catwalks. Bot-speak filling the air.

As her vision cleared, Hoonra could see she was surrounded by bots, the one closest to her still holding its shock prod ready. Behind her, the chamber and catwalks were packed with them. Far too late, Hoonra understood the shape of the trap she'd walked into.

"I want you to know, whatever else, that I'm glad you're here, Hoonra. We have quite a bit to discuss."

Ω

The plaque showed the same short scene over and over again. Omega could see a forge. It had to be one. At one end, a figure stood, hammering and shaping, pouring his intention into the piece before him. The bellows besides the smith were massive, but there was another device that drew Omega's eye. It was like a funnel, set above and behind the working figure, with the narrow end hanging just above the anvil. The wide end reached up, extending past the edge of the plaque. There were designs on the device, stars and constellations. One of the designs looked startlingly like Omega's mark. Whatever the picture was meant

92

to represent, it looked like something that was being added to the smith's work.

Omega spun, scanning the room. He thought he'd heard a noise just now—a voice maybe—but the room was empty. After a moment, he moved on to the next plaque.

The scene here was simple. Omega could see the symbol on his hand clearly at the top of the plaque. Below it, set above a field of moving flame, stood a sword. Anxiety flooded Omega as he saw it, but there was adrenaline as well, a rush that kept him fixated. It was powerful, that thing, elegant and deadly, but more than an object. It made him nervous to think about, but he couldn't look away. Omega fought the compulsion as best he could, but his vision swam, darkening.

When he could see properly again, Omega found himself lying in the aisles between the display pedestals. He jolted upright. The plaque he had just seen was behind him now, a few feet away. He had no idea how he'd moved, but he was facing the monolith.

There was something at play here, that was obvious. If it were a defence mechanism of some kind, he would be dead by now. No, it had to be something in the room that wanted to communicate with him. The plaque had shown the scar on his hand. That exact image. Omega went back to it, but the picture would no longer respond. He moved to the next.

There were many swords in this depiction. Omega could see six figures holding similar blades above their heads. Despite their imperious stance, each face kept changing emotions. Omega could see pride, anger, fear. Above them all, their blades began to change as well. A cat's eye opened at the point where the hilt met the handle on each.

The eyes glowed above the figures below, the slender blades crackling with energy, ensorcelled. As the image began to fade, Omega thought he saw the faces of the men and women holding the swords become frenzied, hysterical, then they were all featureless.

He heard his name this time, he was sure of it. But it wasn't the image that was fading. It was his vision again. He reeled, fighting to stay upright, groping for the walls, but his fingers found nothing. He was spinning now, and felt like he was falling, even though his feet were still under him. He hit something that crumbled beneath his weight, and he staggered. On his knees, Omega's vision began to brighten once more.

The monolith was before him. About halfway up, Omega could see the symbol from his scar. Below that, a portion of blade protruded, the crossguard and handle within reach.

Of course, Omega thought. He reached for the sword hilt.

He felt the other's presence immediately. Like some great hibernating thing, it stirred as he drew the blade. Hefting it, Omega looked at the crossguard as the cat's eye fluttered a little, and then snapped open.

"Awake. Awakened." The voice was in Omega's head, but he felt surrounded by it as well. "Open yourself to me."

Omega's knees buckled, his vision darkening as it had before.

"At last, a seeker to heed my call; another wanderer, tired of the incompetence you see around you. You seek power, crave it. I will make you strong! Know this: I am Kazar-Ky, Lord of Entropy, Betrayal

Incarnate. My brothers and I were given shape and deadly purpose as Ruinblades. The time has come to serve that purpose once more."

"I don't understand."

"You will learn."

Though Omega's body didn't move, he felt himself rising up, his mind flung across time and space.

Ω

Hoonra tested the restraints again, but it was no use. Beside her, two bots remained to activate the devices around her seat. The rest had left after she surrendered.

"They have other jobs to do, now that we have you in place." The Dreamer had remained visible to her throughout the process.

"I can read your thoughts, you know. I did the same thing to Omega when I first met him. You were closed to me then, Hoonra, or I might have guessed your worth." The Dreamer traced the lines of Hoonra's scar. "Things are different now."

"Omega will find me."

"Will he? How? And how do you know my trap didn't kill him after all?" When Hoonra didn't answer, she continued. "Oh, Hoonra. Our beliefs define our reality, don't they? Trust me, I know better than most. Your faith in him is so strong. I have to say, I envy that; gods kill each other for that sort of devotion."

For the first time since her capture, Hoonra met The Dreamer's eyes. "You are no god."

"No? Well, if not, I'm close enough to count." As she spoke, two large pieces of machinery were moved into position at Hoonra's temples. Their humming made the Karackian's head hurt, her vision blur. The Dreamer continued, "There's little point in denying it, my dear. I am your new god, and you my new Avatar. You have been chosen for me." Again, she touched Hoonra's scar.

Hoonra found it difficult to focus. The machines buzzed louder, still picking up speed, and she felt as if she were being pulled into them somehow, her prodigious strength draining away. Through chattering teeth, she strained to speak.

"Omega will—"

"Omega already has, my dear." The Dreamer stepped back as she spoke. It seemed to Hoonra like the rest of the world fell away; she could see only the child now. "Like you, Omega has been chosen to serve a higher purpose."

The Dreamer reached forward to place her open palm on Hoonra's forehead. "To my worshippers, my name is Lyra," she whispered. Hoonra could do nothing to escape her touch. Again, that deep sense of disorientation, but worse; she felt like an insect swept away by a surging river, consumed.

Just when she felt she might lose herself completely, Hoonra heard an explosion. Someone was coming down the catwalk. Despite the strain she felt, she gave a weak laugh. "I told you he'd come."

Lyra removed her hand and scowled. The bots moved out onto the catwalk, lasers ready. Two blasts from a ray-gun sliced through them. As if he'd planned the whole thing from the beginning, Omega leapt into the chamber. Before Lyra could speak, he fired at the pod above

Hoonra. Lyra screamed and disappeared as an electrical fire began spreading through the equipment. The restraints holding Hoonra snapped open.

There was a moment then, just a second, where Hoonra's vision blurred. Despite herself, she was sure it was Lyra, The Dreamer, who stood before her, and not her boss, Omega. She blinked, and her vision cleared.

"This place is coming down; we don't have much time." Omega motioned for her, but Hoonra was up and ready, sword in hand.

"Thank you, Omega."

"Thank me on the *Buccaneer*. Let's get out while it's still an option." The Dreamer mouthed the words as she projected an image of Omega saying them into Hoonra's mind, her hand still resting on the Karackian's head. Lyra smiled as she felt Hoonra accept the vision, falling into a deep slumber fill with dreams of her escape with Omega.

Ω

Omega strode through the carcass of a battle frigate. The wall ahead had been blasted away, and hillocks and craters spread out across the moonscape before him. Other ships had likewise crashed, and the whole field swarmed with combatants.

Omega jumped from the wreckage to land amongst a group of bots, the Ruinblade humming in his hand. He scattered them, firing his ray-gun into one, then another, before swinging Kazar-Ky neatly through a third. The sword howled as it rent the machine, and Omega wasn't sure if he heard metal shearing metal, or the insane laughter of a dead god. He didn't care. When those bots were too mangled to provide any further sport, Omega moved on. Laser blasts glanced off his armour, and Kazar-Ky whispered in his mind.

No more odd jobs for Omega Brown, no more Syndicate contracts, no more getting stranded or haggling for half-assed repairs. No more fixing other people's mistakes. No more need for a bodyguard. With Kazar-Ky at his side, Omega knew he'd have the power to achieve whatever he wanted. The universe would remember the name of Kazar-Ky, and he would reap the rewards.

Omega wasn't sure how long he'd lain on the reliquary floor. Eventually, he'd remembered himself, and stood. There wasn't much time now. Kazar-Ky had warned him about what was coming next. It would be a near thing, but Omega knew he could make it. He left, heading back to the place where he'd seen the bots earlier.

His body felt healed, strong. When he found the checkpoint defended, he did what came naturally. He was among them before they knew he was there, his laughter loud and harsh when he saw the truth of what the Ruinblade promised. He demolished them, and Kazar-Ky propelled his feet over the pile of rubble and out into the Cirellan desert.

He didn't stop until he came to a fissure amongst the rocks. He could feel the sword vibrating in his hand, and figures began to emerge from the hole. They were shifters, and they fell to their knees as soon as they saw the blade. *My faithful servants* echoed through his head, and Omega wondered just how long these things had been out here, waiting.

"Show me my inheritance!" Omega demanded, and the words sounded like two voices speaking at once. The creatures turned to obey, and the man that Omega Brown had become allowed himself to be shown the very dangerous bounty which Kazar-Ky had so carefully hidden beneath the planet's surface.

Ω

Hoonra stared blankly forward. From behind the misted pane of the incubator, the real Lyra considered her prize. She could feel the Karackian sinking more and more deeply into the fantasy she'd created. With her new Avatar secured, she was ready for the final step—and not a moment too soon.

Lyra could no longer sense Omega even vaguely, which meant that he must have found her brother as she'd guessed he would. She would need to hurry if she were to succeed in keeping Kazar-Ky imprisoned in the temple vault.

After she had finally escaped Tellaria, thanks to Omega, Lyra found a way to contact her ancient allies, The Swarm, created by her Sisters long ago. Once reunited with her, they informed her about Omega's encounter on the space station and their own suspicions about the researchers' work. The Swarm had suspected one last great treasure, but even Lyra would never have thought that her brother would entomb his Avatar there for safe keeping.

Kazar-Ky had been so clever. Very few could create an Avatar. One might pass the power to another, or a Lord or Lady might choose to mark a new vassal, but either choice came at the expense of the giver's strength. Lyra had lost her own true Avatar, and so much of her power by the end of the war that she could not create another. She had thought the same of Kazar-Ky. The old monster had outmanoeuvred her. Their conspiracy to control all believers, to subjugate their siblings, had come so close to working the first time, but Kazar-Ky, by his nature,

99

could not be trusted. Of course he'd kept a variable open. Now, inexplicably and after ages, two Avatars recharged the field. She had thought to use Omega, but what did that matter. Hoonra would serve just as well, and if she was fast, Harmony would reign supreme once more.

Lyra could sense the power running through the structure around her, feeding her strength and belief from her most important supplicant. She took a deep breath and, testing the machine, willed her body to change. Once she was transformed into the girl Hoonra had envisioned, she examined herself, pleased.

"Finally, we can begin."

Ω

See Cirella in its final moments before the change, the weal about to burst. It begins in the city foundations. Energy hums, firing though ancient cables, activating long-dormant machines. Soon, entire sections of the foundation begin to vibrate, but only the people of the lower levels sense this disturbance. For them, and everyone else, there is no escape. The buried temple—which is not just a temple—activates its engines, drawing power from the planet's core. Lyra's temple begins to lift, pulling apart Cirella City and destabilizing the planet's surface.

Inside, Lyra can feel her power growing, can sense the panic and pain of thousands of life forms believing in her for the first time in millennia. She grants them a small mercy, wiping their minds to idiocy so that they cannot properly comprehend what comes next. She could save them, but their fear, their belief is so intoxicating, and she's waited so long. Better their deaths serve a purpose.

She reaches out with her thoughts, but the entity she seeks is already in motion. A warship, huge and gothic, heaving up from the desert barrens. She envisions the ship's engines failing, but her Brother is ready. She doesn't know how he summons the strength to defy her, but his ship blasts off, leaving her slower, more encumbered vessel behind.

Lyra's scream is that of a petulant child, and the people of Cirella feel it, crying out even as she does. Kazar-Ky is free.

As Kazar-Ky and Omega's warship enters the atmosphere, Lyra's temple begins its final push. Kilometers of the city are laid to waste as the juggernaut drags debris up with it. Finally, the great pyramid is clear, carving its way back into the wider galaxy.

As Lyra reaches orbit, she loses sense of where her Brother has gone. He's left the system or is just about to, and she knows she will not catch him now. The Gods' War will be renewed.

Lyra turns her attention back to Cirella. Concentrating, drawing on the energy provided by Hoonra, and now by the fear she's created in the planet's citizens, Lyra begins shaping.

Bots were perfectly loyal, deeply obedient, but ultimately unworthy. They had an intelligence of their own, certainly, but the faith produced by weighing statistics and data did not match what a congregation of living souls could do. The people of Cirella would be her new vassals, and Hoonra first among them. They would not be the last.

They would be obedient. They would serve. Lyra would be their new master.

Episode 5:

Kazar-Ky's War

Omega strode into the war-room of the *Deceiver*, the god-blade's voice echoing through his mind. Kazar-Ky's energy was intoxicating. He could feel it surging through his body, like a current beneath his skin. Inside, an assembly of Warlords—*his* Warlords—stood around a hologram in the center of the room. High ceilings in the war-room, and the bright contrast of the hologram against an otherwise dark background, brought their faces into stark relief.

Despite their various species, they all shared similarly grim expressions. He regarded them all, savouring the flow, basking in the power of the weapon at his side. The living cat's eye in the weapon's crossblade stared out, flicking its hungry gaze across everything it could perceive. When he opened his mouth, the god-blade spoke through him. "Where is our prize?"

One of his lesser Warlords, Tr'Khan, replied, "The main bulk of the Swarm fleet has moved, Avatar. They've left a resistance behind to hinder interlopers but seem otherwise unaware of our presence here. The artifacts remain in the Temple."

"Good. Their fleet will not be an issue." As the words left Omega's mouth, it was as if he were only just now thinking of them for the first time. Kazar-Ky moved through him as needed. Provided that he let that happen, Omega could simply hang on for the ride. He wallowed in Kazar-Ky's presence, submerged in the fullness of the ancient being's energy. Soon there would be violence, and the ecstasy the blade brought would crest. Omega clung to each second as Kazar-Ky led.

Across from him, the Warlord Tr'Khan watched in fascination. Bright, yellow eyes set into a dark, lupine face, he was covered head to foot in light combat armour strapped above a coarse, black and rust-red pelt. He stood as tall as Omega, but was knotted in thick muscles, the knees of his powerful legs bent backwards like a pack hunter, long articulate fingers ending with cruel, spiked nails. He was an alpha of his people, born and trained to lead. The Warlord's pack elders had told him stories of the Entropy Lords from millennia ago. Despite his role as a glorified scout here, there was no question in his mind about his place in this war room.

No, what piqued Tr'Khan's interest just now was not the god-blade, nor the battle plan, but rather the scrap of a man Kazar-Ky clung to. It was baffling to Tr'Khan that so spineless a being could come into the possession of so great a weapon. And all because of the mark this fool had caught on his hand. Tr'Khan risked a glance at his own. His people had looked high and low for any trace of a Prime Acolyte, but they were extinct. It had just been a lucky roll of the dice for this lout, really. Right time, right place.

Now, Omega Brown was at the head of an army, joined with Kazar-Ky and made his Avatar, and beneath it, Tr'Khan was sure, was largely ignorant of the real power he held. The blade was using him as a willing puppet, the man a passenger in his own mind. A human rag doll. Tr'Khan fought down a grimace, but the lure of the sword, the sheer intoxication of its presence kept him loyal. He tuned back in when he noticed the rag doll staring at him.

"Yes, Avatar?"

The god-blade spoke again with that thrilling, roaring voice: "Warlord, we await your report."

"Of course, Avatar." Tr'Khan stepped forward and keyed the display. The hologram changed. Now it showed an ice field beneath an overcast sky, a temple complex extending from the field to the mountain range behind. "The relics of Khet lie in three separate locations within the Templar's compound. The first is external, but that won't necessarily make it easier to secure."

The display focused on a huge metal frame which had been built atop a veranda several hundred meters from the Temple doors.

"The removal of Swarm forces from the area will make things easier, but this is where we'll meet the heaviest resistance. This relic is also the largest; while the others can be lifted by hand, the first will require mechanical aid and the destruction of the building beneath it."

"We will lead the assault on each front." The Avatar began speaking almost before Tr'Khan had finished.

Tr'Khan clenched his jaw and waited.

The Avatar took a breath before continuing. "Heavy resistance will not stop us."

"Of course not, Avatar." Even though he knew it was the blade he addressed, it was grating to speak to the face that Kazar-Ky had chosen. "While we know for certain the location of the first relic, the other two remain hidden somewhere within the complex. We believe the second to be somewhere here." The view shifted again, focusing on a middle section of the Temple, without showing anything inside.

"Currently, the third is still beyond us, though we do have some suspicions. The crystal fields in the mountains defy our sensor scans, and thus remain a possible target. Another possibility is the rumour of deep vaults below the Temple. Once we have taken the first relic, things will become much easier; we can use the veranda as a staging point for the rest of our assault. Successfully taking the first relic will provide us with a direct route into deeper parts of the compou—"

"We will lead the main assault, as we have said. Warlord Barthax, your crew will take two transports and follow us down. Once we have created a beachhead, the rest of you may bring your warriors. Go now. Ready your troops."

"Avatar," Tr'Khan called, forcing himself to ignore the other Warlords as they rolled their eyes. Tr'Khan was a leader amongst his own kind, but he knew he was little more than a glorified messenger in the other Warlords' minds.

The Avatar regarded Tr'Khan in very much the same way the Warlord might look upon his own weakest whelp. "What is it, Warlord?"

"This reconnaissance mission was costly. Some of my best did not return." The Avatar said nothing, so Tr'Khan leaned in: "My warriors would not appreciate the message that their best effort has earned them a place in our back ranks."

The other Warlords turned away, hiding their mockery behind the knowing looks they gave each other. The Avatar, alternatively, adopted the posture of a weary parent. He moved around the holographic display until he stood within a foot of Tr'Khan. "Warlord."

"Yes, Avatar."

"Whose warriors?" He spoke in little more than a whisper, and, reaching up gently, placed a hand on Tr'Khan's shoulder.

"...Yours, Avatar."

"Whose message?"

"Yours, Avatar." Tr'Khan stifled a shiver as the Avatar tightened his grip painfully on a handful of Tr'Khan's fur.

"Whose ranks?"

"Yours, Avatar." Tr'Khan balked, his eyes dropping to his feet.

Still holding Tr'Khan, the Avatar raised his voice, "We have given our orders. Go." He turned and left, leaving the rest to file out behind him.

Tr'Khan waited until the end. Shame kept him behind, and it stung, but it wouldn't last. The sword was testing him. The old god could feel his thoughts, and could see he was a better choice than the fool it had become attached to. So what if Tr'Khan didn't have the mark? He just needed to prove himself, and Lord Kazar-Ky would finally choose him instead.

Ω

Omega piloted his troop transport, breaking through the ozone layer and into the frigid atmosphere of the planet before him. This transport was his alone, modified to be independent of the Dreadnought and crewed by one person. He could even slave the other transports to his shuttle's command if he needed to, though he hadn't tried it yet. The Avatar, after all, often needed to take things into his own hands.

Omega felt exhilarated, his flight suit and helmet ready, the power of the god-blade seething in every inch of his being. This was when Omega felt most alive now, when he felt most attuned to Kazar-Ky. In these moments, there was no fighting for control, no waiting for the use of his own body, no vague thoughts and apprehensions while Kazar-Ky was dormant. Here, in the moment of the attack, there was only connection, the old god opening itself fully to him. Conjoined like this, the Avatar was unstoppable.

Omega keyed the controls, preparing a preset escape route. The temple below was still far off, but the ground cannons had already begun hurling neon death. He laughed as the first laser bolts passed, drawing his transport out in a wide arc before cutting sideways across the firing field. He gave the cannons below him a fine look at his flank before spinning the vessel back into a plummeting dive.

The bait worked beautifully. The sky was full of destruction now, but Kazar-Ky's power gave Omega extraordinary speed, and his hands were almost precognitive in their reactions. The transport skipped between the empty spaces, and Omega could see it was nearly time to introduce himself properly. He keyed open the hatch, the straps on his seat shaking as they fought to keep him inside.

At the last possible second, Omega punched the final key sequence and undid his seat straps. His chair tipped him back as he did it, launching him neatly into the pressure stream created by the open door. Once Omega had cleared the portal, the ship banked away, streaking back off in the direction he'd come from.

Omega fell, the momentum of the ship slinging him towards the ground. The guns below fired in confusion, some of them tracking the fleeing vessel while others took potshots at the bizarre projectile he had become. Before him, Omega could see his target: the domed structure atop the great veranda. He flicked his rocket boots on and adjusted his fall to aim for the side of the dome itself.

Omega undid the catch on his scabbard, the skin of his scarred hand itching with anticipation. Despite the windy force of his fall, he drew the god-blade from its sheath. The weapon howled as it cut the air, and Omega brought it before himself. He could feel Kazar-Ky focusing its energy, the blade growing white hot, turning Omega into a bolt of human lightning.

The Avatar's meteoric dive smashed through the dome's side, gouging a rough trough across the cobblestone floor of the veranda beneath. Its defenders didn't know what hit them, couldn't even guess, until the first of them saw a figure leap from the crater to land gracefully at its edge. The few bots present fell first, the Avatar tearing them down as the sword shrieked in his hand. Then he turned to the Temple guard.

When the last defender was slain, the Avatar faced the veranda's arched entrance. Outside, he could see a mass of troops streaming out of the temple towards him: Templars with common bots and, here and there, clusters of Swarm bots. This was the main thrust of their troops. Even without their heavy cannons, the Avatar would have had a difficult time standing against them all. They couldn't have been more obliging of his plans if he'd have asked them himself.

Right on cue, the mass of storm clouds above and behind the temple began disgorging his assault craft. The heavy guns on the surface were bombed to shrapnel, the barrage pausing only long enough for the assault ships to leave the entrance unharmed before dropping the rest of their payload onto the unprotected troops scrambling to get back inside. The few that actually reached the veranda wished they hadn't.

The Avatar could hear his troop carriers landing in the snow fields behind the dome, as the assault ships spun back for another pass. His army had come. He waited for the first of his Warlords to arrive and finish securing their beachhead. The battle was over.

Ω

Months before, back when Omega was still travelling with Hoonra—back before the universe and his place in it were changed irrevocably—he and his bodyguard had been hired to locate some miners who had been lost in a cave system too dangerous for their company to manage. The place had been filled with all sorts of nasty little critters—and a few very large ones—but what made it particularly maddening was the way the tunnels kept leading them back out.

No matter how hard they tried, neither he nor Hoonra could seem to find an entrance which brought them any farther than a few dozen meters into the rock before twisting and turning its way back out to the place they'd entered. Hoonra had been so bothered by this trick that she'd eventually tried to draw a continuous line wherever she went within the caves, just to be sure she wouldn't retrace her steps. It had taken them hours of marking, and remarking, until they'd finally found the only alcove which led farther into the network.

Omega found that the forward command station, which had been erected underneath and around the remains of the veranda, was very much like this. In fact, all of the architecture he had encountered in his new role seemed to fit this description. Though the hallways were

110

lofty, they were not brightly lit. Low track-lights ran along the floors, aided slightly by dim recessed bulbs above. Darker blue and purple tones coloured the walls, seeping out from the corridor paneling, but these did little more than indicate where one could not go. The whole effect was disorienting.

Omega had ordered the shifters, which had stationed themselves in intervals about the place, to increase the brightness or build a series of obvious signs, anything that might help, but the creatures had acted as though they couldn't understand what he spoke about. It was an issue they seemed to suffer from occasionally, and only on particular subjects. He'd let the matter rest.

Omega found himself at a crossroads and stopped. Every direction, including the one behind him, looked identical. When Kazar-Ky controlled him, these tunnels were never a problem, but they became labyrinthine when the blade went dormant.

"You look lost." He hadn't heard Kitt approach, hadn't known she was there until she whispered to him, her hands falling lightly on his shoulders. He jumped and she laughed. "It's just me, oh wise Avatar, no need for alarm. Something on your mind?"

"No, nothing. Well, actually, I was just wondering where you were."

Kitt arched her brow. "Of course." She said nothing else as she took his hand. Certainty flowed from her touch, an affirmation through intimacy which Omega had begun to crave. He followed, as she led him to his quarters.

Later, Omega stood by an image above the table in his private quarters. The projection simulated the space outside Kazar-Ky's ship.

In the near distance, perhaps a few thousand meters out, automated machines bustled around numerous scaffolds.

There were three building sites, so to speak, each connected to the others by steady streams of construction machinery. Zooming in, Omega could see the structure from the veranda being moved into a central place between the sites. Scaffolding was already being constructed to reach it.

Kitt approached, wrapped only in a bedsheet, sliding her arms around his waist. "You're tense." She leaned into his shoulder as she spoke. She had been a companion to him these last few weeks, but Omega was damned if he could remember when, or how exactly, she'd shown up.

Instead of pressing the issue again, he said, "No, just curious. A bit more of that thing gets finished every day. All those artifacts and parts we keep working for." He turned and she looked up at him, concerned.

"What is it?"

Omega smiled, feeling awkward. "It's funny, but it's almost like old Kazar doesn't want me to know." He searched her face. He was admitting, he realized, something that might not be safe, but Kitt gave no sign she was shocked.

It was just that he felt so much trust for her; it was a pull that bordered on instinct. Her eyes were dark, her hair a smoky corona about her face; she drew him always, but he found her hard to focus on. More like a memory or a promise than an actual flesh and blood person.

"I mean, I feel why I need those things when he's with me, you know? When he fills up my mind. But it's like he takes it all with him when he goes. What, uh," he searched for the right words, "what do you think that means?"

"Who cares?" She brought her hands up to his chest. "Let the management worry about things like that."

"The management?"

"I mean the sword. I don't think all those details are worth your time. Put them behind you. I thought you told me you were tired of living with worry."

"I was, but details?" Omega almost laughed, stepping back, "I mean, it seems like a bit more than that, surely. We've been to over a dozen planets across Syndicate space now, looking for these things. I can only imagine what our work has done to some of those places; I know the Syndicate is ineffective, but at least it's stable. And we're disrupting everything. It's true, the Dreamer has to be stopped, but some of the fighting has been pretty intense. It's lucky we only ever fight her bots. If we were out here hurting...people, you know, even if they're enemy soldiers? I don't know." A grimace passed over Omega's face. He rubbed the bridge of his nose with his scarred hand.

"Something wrong, Omega?"

"That last fight. Something I said reminded me of it, but I already lost why. It's just..."

Kitt stroked his face and neck, coaxing him.

"It's hard to keep things straight these days. I guess I want to know what it's for, you know? All this work. All these places we go to stop whatever it is that the Dreamer is working on. And there's something else. All these planets, all these run-ins with her forces and still no sign of Hoonra. It's hard not knowing what's happened to her. I knew her for a long time. If you were me, wouldn't you want that?"

Kitt's answer was simple. She leaned in, pressing her lips to his, guiding his scarred hand gently down.

"I already have what I want. Don't you feel the same way, Omega?"

"I do."

"Then it doesn't matter. Forget it," she whispered, and when she kissed him again, he did.

Ω

The vestibule shook as the invaders broke further into the temple. Inside, four Templars of Khet—the last of their order—finished their prayers and drew their weapons. Electricity hummed down the length of their pulswords as they checked and rechecked the charges. It wouldn't be long now. Nothing had stopped the advance of Entropy's forces. If they must die, it would be fulfilling their posts.

Somewhere outside of their chamber, the last of the temple guards would be making their stand. The hallway leading down to them was heavily fortified, the doorway to this chamber twice reinforced, so the Templars could only measure their enemy's progress by the distant sounds which managed to seep in. That faint, chaotic buzzing, for example, was the report of energy rifles. The growling vibration which followed must be the deployment of the heavy guns. The blast these machines created was an almost constant reverberation.

Then there came a tortured shrieking, as of steel dragged across concrete. The guns went silent. The occasional buzz from the energy rifles again, then nothing. It was time.

The reinforced doors squealed as the end of a blade tore through. White hot and glowing, it rent a molten line across the barrier before disappearing and starting again at the top. A few determined strokes turned the vault door to tatters.

The man holding the weapon, when he finally stepped through, was not whom they had expected. Years of training and commitment to dogma had ingrained in them certain expectations. The Templars had at least assumed their enemy would look the part. Instead, the man before them looked like an average spacer, perhaps even one a little down on his luck. He was covered head to toe in a motley of equipment that had been rigged to work together. Were it not for the blade he held, they might not have believed him at all.

For his part, the spacer ignored them, looking past to peer at the crystalline, pyramidion frame which hung on the wall behind them. Satisfied that it was the object he sought, he turned back towards the hole he'd made. The second his attention shifted, the closest Templar rushed in, silent as a razor, pulsword raised high for a quick kill.

His blow never landed.

The spacer changed almost faster than the eye could follow, his aspect turning from cavalier to predatory in an instant. With one hand he blocked the Templar's swing before pushing the bigger man back into the room. He followed, his feet light and quick beneath him now, the sword tip cutting figure eights in the air, a livid orange cat's eye watching for an opening. As the first Templar regained his footing, the spacer stepped among them, measuring, weighing.

He struck. Though his stance remained loose, his arm was precise. He began to lunge, then snapped his blade tip out in a direction he wasn't looking. The feint caught the unsuspecting Templar just below his gorget. The spacer posed, motionless, regarding the others as their brother collapsed in gurgling agony.

Their composure shattered, two Templars dove forward. They bore down on the swordsman, pulswords and heavy armour churning, but if the spacer was worried, he didn't show it. He didn't even give ground. Decades of training were undone in a moment as the man spun into the charge, parrying the blades with more force than his height and weight suggested he could muster.

There was a flash, a concussive wave of heat, and both Templars were blown backwards, the charred body of the first pinning the other as they fell. The spacer followed, almost on top of them, two quick strikes ensuring neither would rise again. He regarded his last adversary.

"Syril was a consummate warrior, the strongest man I ever knew. He'd never lost a match." It was a stupid thing to say, and the last Templar felt it just after she started. The spacer did not care at all about Syril, but she didn't know what else to do.

"He was riddled with uncertainty." The spacer's voice had a strange, two-toned quality to it, as if two beings spoke with one mouth. "He showed it in the way he carried his blade. He was defined only by his weakness. Come, join him."

The Templar shifted into a defensive stance. "No, you will come to me. I am the last Templar of Khet, the last to protect this relic.

116

I make my stand here, before the final altar. It is my place. Honour demands it."

"The others ran at us in despair." The swordsman spoke slowly now, observing. "They saw what we did to the first of you, and they knew they could not win. They charged to speed the inevitable." The spacer paused. It was hard for the Templar to tell because of his helmet, but it seemed, when the spacer spoke again, his voice was changing, almost thinning, becoming singular. "You're younger than they were." It wasn't a question.

The Templar flustered a little. "My age is irrelevant. I am a Templar of Khet, the very last, and I'll not—"

"It's your ideals, I mean. You still care about this, still believe in it. You're not like the last two." Now his voice had shrunk, until it seemed to be just an ordinary man behind that mask and not a monster at all. He lowered his weapon.

"No, I'm not," she shot back through gritted teeth. "I'm better."

"Oh, come on. Of all people, I know a boast when I hear one. You're the last because you still truly carry the faith."

"That's not true. Th-they believed." The Last Templar of Khet, confused by this new tactic, felt herself floundering. "Of course they did. They were two of the best—"

"You looked up to them." Again, not a question.

"Well, I mean, of course I did, I—"

"But you don't need them. You never did." The spacer stepped forward, weapon still lowered. His voice had taken on an almost pleading, apologetic quality. "You've always been stronger than they. Smarter. Faster. More faithful. You followed them because they offered you a path to something new, but staying with them has only dragged you down. Hoonra, I—"

"What's 'Hoon Rha'? the Templar asked. Then: "We've spoken long enough."

The Templar raised her weapon once more, but the spacer no longer seemed to be listening. His head sat askew on his shoulders, as though he was looking at something far away. He started to shake a little and cried out, doubling over, his free hand clutching the back of the other. That fist was locked, the sword quivering in his grip. The paroxysm lasted only a second, but when it passed, the Templar once more faced the monster that had ripped its way into the vestibule. Again, The Last Templar of Khet offered a defensive stance.

This time, the monster obliged.

Ω

By the time Tr'Khan pushed his way into the vestibule, the artifact had already been taken away; a blank space was all that remained where the cap had once been. Everyone else had come and gone, but the Avatar remained. He was standing now as he had been throughout the entire extraction process, staring down at the corpse of a young Templar. Tr'Khan could hear the Avatar's heavy breathing even from beneath his helmet. He seemed to sway a little on his feet. Had the others simply left him like this? The Warlord approached cautiously.

"Avatar, this complex is vast, bigger even than our initial reports suspected, but we have found the final vaults, deep below us. There will be a few more pockets of resistance, but the last artifact is within reach." He waited for an answer. "Avatar?"

"Who was this?" The unholy harmony of the Avatar's voice had broken, the two tones now impressing, now guttering, like two people shouting out the same sentence from different rooms.

Tr'Khan stifled his reaction. No wonder the others had left the Avatar alone; he sounded broken and, Tr'Khan thought, weak.

"A Templar, Avatar. The other Warlords said you made short work of them."

The Avatar looked back down. Again, that faint swaying, but now Tr'Khan saw something else: the Avatar's sword hand quivered, the cat's eye in the weapon's pommel half-lidded. It seemed that the Avatar's grip was relaxing, muscle by muscle, the sword shaking free. As he watched, the blade slid, just slightly, in his grip.

Tr'Khan reached out almost without thinking. His claw drew within an inch of Kazar-Ky before the Avatar's other hand landed an open slap across his face. Despite the man's relative size, Tr'Khan crumpled, his head ringing. When he finally managed to roll to his side, he found Kazar-Ky's tip pressed against the pit of his throat. The demon-god's cat's eye blazed in its crossguard. Any second now, Tr'Khan knew, that cold and hungry blade would slice neatly in, parting the skin and hair like creased paper. He wondered if he'd even properly feel it.

The moment stretched.

Without a word, the Avatar backed away, Kazar-Ky still trained on Tr'Khan. The Warlord watched as the Avatar sidestepped to the vestibule's entrance and slipped from the room.

Tr'Khan remained where he was, contemplating the doorway, a portal through which his guaranteed death had, inexplicably, decided to exit.

But of course, it wasn't inexplicable. The answer was obvious.

The Avatar had promised death, then hesitated.

It was time.

Ω

Kitt found Omega in his own quarters. When she entered, he was examining the progress of the machine in orbit, his back to her. The scaffolds had come together around the newly-acquired artifacts. The whole thing was beginning to resemble a dish with an antenna.

"Avatar?"

"Not right now, no. Do you need to speak with him about something?" There was an edge in Omega's tone that stopped her.

"Oh, sorry, Omega, I just...I guess I'm not used to you finding your way here alone."

"Not used to me finding my way to my own room?" He sounded like he'd say more, but didn't. Then, quietly, "It's true, I'm hardly ever on my own anymore. Between the Warlords, you, old Kazar..."

Kitt could see his belt and the sword lying on his bed, its cat's eye closed, sleeping.

"I honestly can't remember the last time I had a true moment alone. We're almost done with this thing, aren't we?" He motioned to the hologram on the wall.

"I wouldn't know."

Finally, Omega turned. Kitt's first thought was that he'd been crying, his face puffy and graceless. She didn't notice the look he gave her until a moment later. Clearly, Omega saw something he wasn't sure he liked.

"I think that you do. I think that I share a lot of what I know with you, and you don't share all that much back."

"What are you talking about?"

"You look different today, Kitt."

"Nothing's changed."

"No," Omega gave a shaky grin and sniffled, "that's not true. Something *is* different. I took Kazar off today. Can't actually remember the last time I've done that on my own. Just took off the belt and left him there. My scar's been burning ever since." Omega's voice had began to rise as he spoke, his scarred hand rising with it, as if in testimony: "It's been burning all morning. Funny thing is, that's not the only time. Once I started thinking about it, it seemed like my hand hurt every time I saw or remembered something Kazar-Ky didn't like. Why do you suppose that is, Kitt? For someone who doesn't know anything, I also can't help but notice it always hurts a little less around you."

"That's because I'm here to help!" Kitt tried to rush in, but Omega moved, putting the projector and table between them. He was pressed back against the wall.

"Okay," she said, "okay. Let's talk. We actually do talk pretty often, though you generally don't remember—and I am actually here to help." She moved across the sitting area to the other side of the room, and sat on the corner of the bed. The doorway was now empty. Omega understood her message, but stayed by the wall.

"You're right, we are almost finished." Kitt nodded over to the holo on the wall. "You've secured the last artifact; we've had the third one all along. It's impossible to replicate the parts any longer. The infrastructure just doesn't exist, or the science. Gathering up the pieces like this really is the best way."

"To do what?"

"To let the others back in, Omega," Kitt tilted her head, her tone implying that the answer should be obvious, "to bring Kazar-Ky's brothers back from the other side."

Omega nodded, his expression grim. "To forge weapons for the other Warlords."

Kitt laughed at this. "No. No other god-blades, Omega. I wasn't kidding when I said that the infrastructure is gone. Lord Kazar-Ky is the last of its kind. Believe it or not, but you really did manage to luck your way into bearing the last mark that could match with him."

"Then what do the other warlords want with Kazar's brothers?"

"I couldn't say. Some of them are truly faithful, you know, if a bit blind, but most are just looking for profit. I don't think that any of them have really thought through what this thing will do. They can't see past the power you wield."

Unconsciously, Omega moved away from the wall. It was working, as Kitt knew it would, as it had done in the past. She just needed him a bit closer.

"If you think so little of them, why serve them against me?" There it was, and just a little faster than usual this time around. Kitt could see the vacant look returning to Omega's eyes as he drew nearer the bed.

"I don't serve them."

"No, you don't." Omega looked confused now, like he was trying to remember something more. "You told me already. You serve—"

"Kazar-Ky," Kitt finished for him, and rose. Omega twitched a little at her motion, and she kept her distance. "Warlords come and go. Some of us though—some of us have been serving Kazar-Ky and the Lords of Entropy for time out of mind. To his most faithful servants, to me, your coming was like a forgotten promise, finally remembered." Her voice was smooth, her hips rocking just so as she spoke. "Lord Kazar-Ky gave me my life. He needs me. And now he needs you too. I owe everything to him; as Avatar, that's your due as well."

She stepped forward confidently now, one arm slipping across his shoulder, the other around his waist. Omega tried to look at her, but after a moment his eyes wandered the room, unfocused.

"He needs the mark?" Omega forced the words around a thick tongue.

Kitt rewarded him with a look of actual surprise. "Well done, Avatar. We've had this conversation half a dozen times now, but that's the first time you've locked everything into place. That's right, Lord Kazar-Ky needs the mark. It's how you two 'mesh together', if you like. You do his work, and he grants you extraordinary privilege. All you have to do is go along for the ride."

She leaned up close to Omega's face, burying him in her hair and her body's natural perfume, her lips close. "These last few missions have been hard on our Master, and he's become more dormant than usual. That's why you're having all these awful, confusing thoughts. It's happened before. Don't worry. Soon he'll be rested, and you can go back to forgetting."

Omega pulled back a little at this, bewildered. "Am I a prisoner here?"

"If you are, does that mean you can't enjoy it?" She drew him in again, kissing his mouth to silence him.

Omega felt overwhelmed. The woman before him was soft and willing, driving every other thought from his mind, but there was something else. Another face. Another woman who appeared every time he tried to picture the one holding him. A Templar, whom he'd killed in cold blood for the audacity of believing in something more than herself.

Her, and one other equally dedicated to her sense of honour, whom he'd also left behind. Abandoned, he saw now, likely when she'd needed him most.

Kitt pulled him towards the bed, but Omega didn't move, his emotions churning. When he looked down at her, he gasped. Kitt's words still clung to his mind, and as he heard them again now, he saw her with fresh eyes. Her features weren't smoky or dark, they were ill-defined. Her eyes were more like dots on a moth's wing, her hair not a corona but a knot of seething ends. Her features were lumpen, almost waxy, and it looked as though her body was a collection of thick cords bound together, instead of proper muscle and sinew.

The shifter that Omega knew as Kitt split its head, bleating out a sort of laugh. Omega felt sick. "We all serve the Master," it howled before bearing down, twisting about his legs and hips, entangling him.

The pair dashed the table over as they fell, Omega flailing his arms while the thing he had called Kitt tried to immobilize him. It wouldn't kill him, he realized, just keep him stuck until Kazar-Ky was ready. He could feel the god-blade stirring, far in the back of his mind. It wouldn't be long now. Kitt continued to engulf him, moving up his body like some kind of fleshy tar. On the ground by his head, Omega's hands latched onto the fallen holo projector.

Omega smashed the machine into the shifter's head, catching it by surprise. He swung again as the creature tried to change its body into something more defensible, but a chunk of screen shattered off, causing it to howl. Omega kept thrashing, driving the equipment down until he felt the glove enveloping him become loose. Scrambling, he extricated himself from the body.

He didn't know if the shifter was dead or just unconscious, but it didn't matter. Kazar-Ky was waking up. He could feel the presence in his mind growing, battening itself onto his own thoughts, forcing his arm to pick up the sword. He couldn't stop it.

The mark. All of this revolved around the mark. Gritting his teeth and clinging to the pain he felt in the back of his hand, Omega grasped the sword.

"SLAVE!" Kazar-Ky's words were as much a sound in his head as they were a physical force, pushing him to the floor. "How dare you defy your station? There is no end to your servitude, Omega Brown. You belong to me!"

The cat's eye glared. Omega felt himself deflating, as if his mind's eye were being stuffed backwards down a long tube, the sight of the room receding, slowly fading farther and farther away. All that was left was his consciousness, the current, and the screaming voice of Kazar-Ky. Each time the god-blade spoke, the pain spiked through him. The old god directed it, smothering him. Letting Kazar-Ky take him was the only way to make it stop.

And he wanted it to stop. He wanted to turn away from it, to let himself be buried by it until he could forget. It's what he'd wanted ever since he got the mark. It's what had put him here in the first place. Running, planning the escape that was most profitable, Omega realized, was the only thing he was ever any good at.

Hoonra had been the one to remind him of duty. Hoonra was the one who always took the harder road. The pain continued sawing through him, but instead of crumbling away, Omega embraced the only choice aside from annihilation. He stood his ground.

It wasn't a sensation he could describe accurately, as it wasn't a thing he physically did. He felt, in his mind, the presence of the god-blade flattening him into nothingness with the pain it wielded. He thought again of Hoonra, how the Karackian viewed every moment of hurt as an opportunity to grow stronger, to push herself to become better.

Omega refused to be undone, his defiance becoming an insulator for the burn, dampening Kazar-Ky's presence. The pain remained intense and acerbic, but it became an affirmation of self, too, a connection to the god-blade which Kazar-Ky could not break. Omega ground his teeth.

"You're going to need to do better than that, old son." Even as he hissed the words, Kazar-Ky's voice came shrieking back to prominence, the conscious meanings replaced by a hateful, wordless scream. It nearly obliterated Omega right then and there but again he thought of his good and only friend.

Hoonra would choose to fight. Hoonra would stand and take the beating, and beat right back. Hoonra would have found a way.

Shouting himself now, Omega stood. His legs locked as he rose, and he hunched over the blade. His body felt rigid, as if held by a strong electric current, but there was balance there, an equilibrium composed of himself, Kazar-Ky, and the pain between them. The god-blade kept howling, but Omega could stand it.

"That's all you can do, isn't it? Shout and howl and hurt, but you've never been held by someone who didn't want you, have you?"

The blade babbled a stream of vitriol into Omega's mind:

"—NOTHING WHEN YOU FOUND ME, NOTHING! YOU WERE WEAK, AND I MADE YOU STRONG, PATHETIC BUT I MADE YOU PROUD! YOU DARE NOT USE ME, DARE NOT, DARE NOT SPEAK—"

The voice kept going but Omega wouldn't hear it. A thought struck him. "The mark is the key, isn't it, Kazar? It's your symbol, but it's in my skin. Mine, so I guess that makes it my symbol too." As he spoke, he felt the balance shift. The pain remained, but Kazar-Ky's voice quieted, even if only a little. The god-blade, it seemed, could no longer simply speak over him if it wished

Omega stood, his limbs unlocking. The sword continued to keen, the god-blade's presence still pushing against his will, but Omega endured. There was no more running from this. It would only let the god-blade back in control, and that would be fatal. Whatever else, Omega Brown was done running away. "If I'm a part of you now, Oh Great and Mighty Kazar-Ky, then I guess that makes you a part of me too. I might not be very good, but I make my own way. Pay my own debts. Because of you, there are people I need to pay back."

The sword quivered in his hand a little; the keening lessened. He could feel the old god in his mind, still a menacing presence, but as if behind glass; like a poisonous snake, Omega knew that Kazar-Ky could still kill him if mishandled. Concentrating, Omega embraced this knowledge, taking the power from the god-blade and pushing him back into dormancy. The cat's eye fluttered, and closed. He slid the sword into its scabbard, the pain lessening, though never fully going away.

The mass on the floor spasmed. Small rivulets of flesh began dribbling up the limbs of the shifter's body, collecting on its torso. It was still alive despite its head injury, and Omega guessed it wouldn't be long before he had to figure out a new way to kill it. There was no time for that. The mark gave him the power, but the sword was the key. Omega could see now that Tr'Khan's reports were wrong. He knew what the third artifact must be. He scrambled, collecting his gear while Kitt continued to regenerate. Just as it began to pile itself upright once more, Omega reached the door to his rooms. If he hurried, there might still be time to do what needed to be done.

Ω

The pit Omega had chosen to wait in was, mercifully, less exposed to the cold than the plateau above it. The wind howled over the edge of its incline, but at the bottom, most of that fury was dulled. Down there, the snow hung in curtains which drifted without ever seeming to fall properly.

Omega hadn't wanted to be down there, hadn't wanted to get out of his ship at all, actually, but circumstances for him had once again changed. Luckily, he was certain he wouldn't have long to wait. Kazar-Ky was still a veritable thorn in his side, but he seemed to have willed the blade into a watchful peace. As long as he kept thinking about the mark and the sensation it created, he could keep control. He paced for a moment around a cluster of huge crystals which jutted up from the centre of the ravine floor beside him, trying his best to keep the blood flowing.

It was only a moment or two later that Tr'Khan arrived. The Warlord moved decisively against the drifts, cresting the edge and descending in a few huge strides, clawed feet gripping the ice. Without looking up, he called out as he went. "And so, I've found the fool at last."

"Don't you mean the *Avatar*?" Omega's response bore all of his usual sarcasm, but even so, he made a point of keeping a safe distance from the canid Warlord. "Where are all your friends?"

129

"My troops await my return as Avatar, onboard the Deceiver. You've caused quite a scene. The other Warlords started fighting once they realized you'd left with most of the troop transports. They're too stupid to see through your ruse, and I wasn't about to enlighten them. A few followed the ship obviously marked as yours, but I do not need or want their help to deal with you."

Omega nodded, impressed. "They fell for the fraud, but you figured out I switched the call signs on the ships. Well done. I have to say, Tr'Khan, I'd always assumed you were too dull to catch something like that. So, you've come to stop me from destroying the third artifact, but you're too late. I've rigged this whole valley with explosives. One touch and every crystal in this range goes straight into the atmosphere."

Tr'Khan was shaking his head even before Omega finished. "No. More lies. You haven't rigged the valley." The Warlord reached out, grabbing one of the crystals and breaking an end off before throwing it to the ground. "These crystals mean nothing. The final relic isn't a part of these crystal growths, and the vaults we found are empty. It's the blade."

Omega gave no response, so Tr'Khan continued, "The shifters took command almost as soon as you left. They were desperate for the sword to be returned. Panicked. I've never seen them act like that. They threatened to destroy us if we didn't fall in line. If they can truly dispose of us, it's either because we've done all they needed, or because nothing but the blade matters. When I am Avatar, I will wring their secrets from them."

"You said 'more lies'. What's the other one?"

"You came here to hide," Tr'Khan sneered. "You hoped that the natural interference created by the crystals would hide your sensor signature. I mightn't have noticed if I hadn't guessed about the call sign change."

"Huh. And you say that you haven't told the others because you...?"

"The glory of your death will be as an opening chorus in the song of my bloody ascension!"

"Right, right," Omega made a winding motion with his hand, "gloriously bloody ascension, got it. And that'll be the reason why you also didn't just destroy my ship when you flew by, right? All that deep tactical thinking you've committed yourself to? Honestly, it's frustrating, Tr'Khan, that you've figured out enough to inconvenience me, yet you still remain so predictably stupid."

The Warlord snarled, but Omega pressed through, "You *are* right about the sword, mind you. I had an experience that convinced me of the same thing. You're right about the call signs, too, but you're only half right about the location. It's true, I *was* using the crystals to hide, just not from you."

Omega glanced at his wrist display and shrugged. "Actually, I thought they'd be here by now, so you'll just have to take my word for—" He looked up suddenly, over Tr'Khan's head, up over the edge of the ravine. "Oh, that's handy. Dramatic, even." Omega pointed.

The Warlord glanced back, then spun and looked again. Just above the ledge, far back and obscured by clouds, Tr'Khan could make out the shape of a Swarm war frigate in the upper atmosphere. The dark clouds billowing from beneath it were far more likely to be waves of bot fighters than just more bad weather.

"I guess none of you managed to figure out that I had a quick look at our comms system on my way out the door. Thought maybe I'd better let someone know we were here."

Tr'Khan turned back around, his chest heaving, drool streaming from the corners of his muzzle. He growled in a way that Omega could feel in his chest. "Good thing you left your warriors up there. They'll be much easier for the bots to find that way. Oh—you can't tell, because of my helmet, but I winked at you when I said that."

Omega rolled his shoulders a little, shaking his hands and setting his feet. "Before we do this, Tr'Khan, I just want you to know: I really don't like you."

Tr'Khan snarled and leaped into the air, drawing two long knives as he did, bridging the distance between them as though it were only a few feet. He brought the blades down in a sweeping arc, and Omega was able to draw Kazar-Ky only just in time to counter them. The demon-god's presence flared again in his mind, and Omega had to fight for control. Between the old god's pressure and the Warlord's assault, he was brought to his knees in an instant.

Leveraging his full weight onto the knives, Tr'Khan leaned forward, "Look at you. Our lord betrays you. Even now, he works to secure my victory."

Omega's arm shook. "What would you do, Tr'Khan, if I gave you the sword here and now?"

"What would I do?" The question excited Tr'Khan enough that Omega could swear he saw the Warlord's eyes bulge a little in their sockets. "I'd burn a thousand worlds. I'd bring the universe to its knees. My people would rule everything in Kazar-Ky's name."

He lifted his head to the sky, feeling Omega buckle a little further as he did it. "I would be the Avatar, Entropy Incarnate, and no mortal could ever stand before me!" Tr'Khan was salivating again as he looked back to Omega, a mad, animal light glimmering in his eyes. This turned quickly into a look of confusion as he noticed the ray-gun Omega had pointed at his chest.

The force of the blast lifted Tr'Khan up and back, only a step or two, but it was enough. Omega stood and slid the sword back into its scabbard. He seemed to regain a little more control then, but through it all, the hand with the gun never wavered. Tr'Khan stared at him, agog, as Omega motioned to the hole in his adversary's chest.

"Predictably stupid," he repeated, "and, if I might add, quite clichéd as well. 'Bring the universe to its knees?' What does that even mean? It doesn't have legs, Tr'Khan." The Warlord seemed to be building up to some kind of response, but Omega couldn't be bothered. He fired again, twice, then left the little valley and the smoking ruin behind him.

Omega had set his vessel to partial standby when he'd left to deal with Tr'Khan, so startup was easy. In moments, he was airborne, skimming along the crystal fields and putting as much distance between him and the extraordinarily messy fight he'd caused back at the temple. He was certain no more of his ex-crew would notice him leaving now, but there was still a Swarm frigate in orbit, and that could certainly be a problem.

Sure enough, Omega's long-range scanners registered a trio of bot fighters moving away from the main battle to investigate the crystal fields shortly after he'd launched.

Time for his final trick. Omega keyed in a preprogrammed sequence. He watched his scanners and saw the remaining transport ships still slaved to his vessel's control. These began their maneuver. Like his own vessel, they were built for speed instead of combat, but it was all he'd need. The transports lifted off, angling themselves in self-destruct runs at any meaningful Swarm target. The distraction worked. Far behind him, the bot fighters swung back to deal with this new threat.

As soon as he felt safe, Omega pointed his ship starward and broke the atmosphere. The Swarm would see him now for sure, but his lead was too great. Omega brought up the coordinates for a close hyperjump.

"I'm sorry," he whispered, "I'm sorry, Hoonra. I'm sorry, and I'm coming back. Hang on." With one last flick of the controls, Omega Brown jumped to hyperspace.

Episode 6:

The Dreamer's Realm

In the early morning light of a war ravaged planet, Omega watched the alien boy begin his day. The boy was lost in a waking dream. As Omega observed him, the youth stumbled through an alley, barely conscious of the blasted stonework he climbed with stork-like feet. He passed through the carcass of a building and on towards the edge of the encroaching forest, where Omega hid on the other side. His pantomime never stopped, and he whispered and clucked with his beak-shaped mouth, talking to companions only he could see.

From within the brush, Omega also watched the lupine predator he hoped to save the boy from. It had been hunting these people for days and Omega had finally managed to sneak up on it. He did his best to move silently closer, but leaves crunching on the forest floor underfoot gave him away. The beast glanced from its prey, then turned, snarling.

"Ah. You weren't supposed to know I was here. I've really got to get better at this whole hunting and tracking thing."

Omega steadied himself as the canid squared with him. In his head, the trammelled voice of Kazar-Ky called out a challenge, urging him to use the sword on his back. Omega did his best to ignore this, focusing on the animal instead. He drew and fired as the beast pounced, two hundred pounds of muscle, teeth, and claws turning to dead weight as his bolt struck home. Omega crashed backwards, landing painfully on a root as the beast's corpse came to settle across him.

He couldn't feel any serious injuries, but it was still a few minutes before he could writhe his way out. By the time he had, the child was gone. As the distant, red sun rose higher, Omega began dragging the corpse back to his camp. The undergrowth was thick, and he cursed himself for not bringing his skinning tools along. In the end, he resorted to hacking off as much of the two powerful hind legs that he could, leaving the rest for another trip.

Arms aching, Omega dropped his load off and returned to the body by mid-morning. In that time, some other, even meaner, thing had found it, and ate as much of it as possible before hauling the rest away. Omega sighed. Opportunities to get fresh meat like this were rare. The snares he'd taught himself to make were useless. He'd only managed to catch this predator because it was distracted. After taking a few minutes to fight down his frustration, he began trekking back to his transport once again.

His transport. For the last few weeks, it had served Omega as a makeshift house and base of operations but he still couldn't think of the retrofitted troop ship as his. In truth, soon he likely wouldn't have to. It was designed for short flights in heavy fighting, not exploration. Omega was sure that coaxing its now worn out hyperdrive into too many more jumps would result in his being vaporized along with the ship.

Omega keyed the controls for entry. Inside were the legs he'd managed to butcher, draining above a wash basin, as well as the other meager supplies he'd scavenged during his stops so far. A few tattered blankets, a stolen cooking unit, some corroded pots, and the basin were most of the possessions he had now.

Omega considered the haunches again. They were well-muscled, and gamey, but there was lots of meat on the bone. He brought them outside, along with the scavenged knives that had become his skinning tools, and did his best. After that, he set about making a spit. It was past midday by now. He'd need to work quickly if he was going to get the meat ready in time.

Ω

The avian boy wandered the shattered city. Still lost in a dreamscape, he followed his nose. As Omega watched from ruins farther down the street, he could see the child making a more or less direct line for the cooked meat he'd left nearby. The boy would find it and bring it back to the other refugees, as he had before. Omega didn't know if these aliens would normally eat a thing like the wolf-beast he'd prepared, but his caring for them had become a routine, and they certainly seemed omnivorous enough to give it a try. As the boy began to carry the plank the food had been set on, Omega sat back against the broken wall, watching the sunset.

It had been the children that made him start doing this. He never planned on becoming a support worker for refugees of the Gods'-War, but once he'd seen the state they lived in, he couldn't ignore it. He had done this to them as the Avatar of Kazar-Ky, back before he'd learned to control the Ruinblade and the old-god trapped inside it. He tried not to think about that. Instead, he pictured the scene behind him now. The boy would be back among his relatives and neighbors. Like him, they would all be distracted, trapped in the waking dreamstate, but the smell of food so close would bring them partially around.

Despite how little of it he could recall, the renewal of the Gods'-War had been terrible for the ordinary people of the galaxy. Omega's first encounter with the aftermath happened shortly after fleeing from his own fleet. Lyra, the creature her faithful called The Dreamer, had since expanded her territory and influence. As he traveled, Omega had found worlds scorched by war, full of survivors locked in hallucination. They lived, all of them, in a sort of waking delusion, a state of altered perception. Omega was spared, he assumed, because of his connection with Kazar-Ky. When he encountered Dreamers up close, they invariably became hostile. He had seen this transformation on the first planet he'd tried, the community there attacking him as one. It was a miracle none of them had been holding anything heavy or sharp. He'd torn himself free of the mob by luck and ran for his ship. They'd followed after him at first, but the deep illusion of The Dream set in again after he'd put some distance between them, and they'd given up.

Omega had rested for a while after this, ultimately deciding on moving to a different planet to try again. It was a lucky thing he did. As he'd left orbit and prepared for his next hyper jump, a Swarm frigate had entered the planetary system. His sensors could read it moving towards him almost as soon as it arrived. It wasn't a coincidence. The Dream wasn't just functioning as a form of population control, it was a warning system as well. The Swarm served The Dreamer. Omega made sure to jump, and jump again before stopping. The Swarm wouldn't relent now that they knew about his presence, even if they weren't sure yet what they were chasing. If Omega wanted to find Hoonra, it was critical that the Swarm didn't get to him first.

Three separate systems now, and over half a dozen planets. His food had run out quickly, his water almost as fast, and the last of his energy crystals had nearly lost their charge. His rocket boots and helmet functions had begun to run down too, wear and tear taking a toll without the supplies to repair them. He'd searched and sneaked and essentially driven himself to starvation, and he still had not the slightest hint where Hoonra might be. He had no idea how to find The Dreamer's temple ship without exposing himself, and even fewer thoughts about how he might go about extracting Hoonra, even if he found her there. He didn't want to admit it, but the truth was that Omega didn't really have any plan at all, aside from begging Hoonra for forgiveness.

When the sun set, Omega stood and stretched. Using the cover of the ruins, he moved to another vantage point: a partially intact roof which overlooked the street he'd just been on. From here, he had an angle into the broken enclosure the boy had returned to. The child stood beside another youngster a few inches shorter, with an older figure nearby. They seemed to be a little unit. Just now, they were huddled together, eating as a family might. Omega found himself smiling as he watched. The two children were gobbling hungrily, and despite their hallucinatory state, they seemed to be enjoying each other's company. Omega wondered if they all experienced the same dream. Whatever they saw in their own minds, whatever rendition of the wreckage about themselves they comprehended, they were at least comforted by one another. He lay on the rooftop well into the night, waiting for them to fall asleep before venturing back to his transport.

Ω

Omega was out early the next morning, checking the tangle of knots he generously referred to as his traps, when he heard a wailing, honking sound coming from the direction of the ruined city. He followed it, and after reorienting himself in the woods a few times, he came to a section of forest that he hadn't yet explored. When he saw the source of the sound, he nearly shouted too.

Ahead of him, just at the edge of the clearing, Omega could see two avian adults fighting for their lives. A six-legged beast, nearly as big as Omega's transport, was toying with them, fascinated by their inability to run farther than a few meters before becoming distracted again. After a moment, the caprine monstrosity pounced, and Omega could hear bones cracking. He looked away, thinking of the child he'd saved from a similar fate. He had done this. He had savaged their planet as the Avatar. He had left them vulnerable to the power which enfeebled them now. Omega moved out of sight as the creature took its second victim, shuddering to think what their hallucination must be showing them. The smaller beasts on this planet were one thing; this creature was something else. It needed to be stopped, but he would need to prepare first if he was going to stop it.

Omega returned to his transport. He had no idea how effective his ray-gun would be, but he strapped it on. His flight suit and tech were still somewhat serviceable, and he hung his sword from his back as he departed once more. He would need to draw on Kazar-Ky's power, but doing so without reservation would turn him back into the Avatar, and Omega couldn't take that risk. As ready as he could be, Omega returned to the scene.

The beast had moved on, the signs of its passing obvious even for someone as inexperienced as Omega. He followed. The trail meandered somewhat, but kept a mostly consistent path bearing south, which ended in a swath of knocked over trees around a cave entrance at the base of a cliff. Standing at the clearing edge, he could hear a deep rumbling emanating from the crack in the cliff face. It was snoring, or breathing heavily at least, after its meal. Having found it, Omega was reluctant to step inside. He looked up, wondering if he could simply find something to block the entrance. That was when another sound caught his ear.

This one was higher pitched than the last, and just as he realized what it was, he saw the two Swarm bot fighters shoot overhead on their way to a landing spot far behind him.

Omega felt as though a hand had reached up from the earth, and pulled the pit of his stomach back down with it. The Swarm had found him. Their trajectory suggested they were already aware of his landing site. He spun, running like mad, through the trees, past the outskirts of the city, and almost back to the transport before he caught himself.

It was too late already. It had to be. The bots had disappeared from the sky long before he'd cleared the trees. Omega leaned against a trunk, breathing in ragged gasps, forcing himself to think. After a moment's consideration, he jogged forward, slowing as he neared his landing site, catching a glimpse of his transport through the trees. He listened. The forest itself had become quiet, and Omega could make out the humming, blipping garble through which the Swarm spoke. Moving further still, Omega could see them through the leaves and branches. From his vantage he could make out four. In his mind, Kazar-Ky urged violence. With the old-god's help, these few wouldn't be a problem. Alternatively, he could wait, try to find the patrols, and take those bots out first. But if that didn't work, or if he wasn't fast enough, the bots around his ship would be notified. Neither of these was a particularly enticing option. Kazar-Ky pushed him again, and Omega thought of his vessel. He didn't know if they'd already tampered with it, but giving them more time to begin wasn't a good idea. He decided his only hope lay in forward momentum and surprise. Omega drew his ray-gun and pulled Kazar-Ky from its sheath, concentrating on the pain he felt in the mark on his hand, summoning the old-god into service.

In the clearing, the bots continued their patrol. One watched the forest while its companions turned to investigate the ship. The first had picked up some rustling in the trees by the clearing's edge. The bot swiveled its head around and scanned the area again, detecting the glint of something metallic in the bushes. It switched to infrared body-heat imaging. The day had become hot, making the blob hiding in the bushes indistinct in its aspect. This issue corrected itself as the shape became humanoid, and sprinted out of the foliage towards it. The bot managed one bewildered squawk before a ray bolt melted a hole through its body.

Omega fired again, cutting a molten tear across his target. As it toppled down, he raised Kazar-Ky, the sword's malign voice echoing through his mind, the cat's eye in the crossguard open and glowing with a baleful orange light. The blade burned white-hot, and he brought it down in a heavy arc, shearing the machine which had just turned from his vessel. Another bot crossed back around, and he ran it through as well, before a bolt hit his calf from behind. He fell, shouting, and rolled beneath the transport's landing struts. From there, he fired his ray-gun at the tripod feet of the final bot, knocking it over before drilling a hole through its side.

His calf hurt, but the pain wasn't debilitating. The shot had probably been hurried. He could treat it inside the ship, and thought he could still try to stand on it. He'd need to if he was going to reach the controls for the door. Omega began crawling back to the edge when he heard a tremendous roaring overhead. His heart skipped. Another ship had passed by, and he cursed his luck. As he got to his knees he could hear the newcomer coming closer, below the horizon of the treeline, blasting a space clear for a landing.

Of course they'd have brought reinforcements. The patrol by his ship was just bait. Luring them away from the site had always been the best idea. In his panic, Kazar-Ky had pushed him in the direction it had wanted. Omega tried to stand, but the burn in his calf muscle hobbled him. He drew on the sword's power, dulling the pain, ignoring Kazar-Ky's laughter, and stood.

He managed to punch two of the numbers in the code before a laser blast smacked into the hull beside his hand. Startled, he spun and dropped again, barely dodging a barrage of energy that battered the ship and reduced the door's keypad to smoking wires and a shattered screen. The bot patrol had returned. He could see them at the forest's edge, another four, pinning him down. He scrambled back beneath the transport. The bots by the trees began advancing, which was bad, but he was more worried about the reinforcements which had landed behind them. He had a few more seconds, maybe a minute, to find a reasonable diversion before the whole clearing would be filled with trigger happy robots looking to fry him.

In his mind, he could hear the old-god in the sword mocking him, offering all the power he'd need and more, if he would just submit. Omega pushed this sensation away, looking around desperately for any kind of solution. He began crawling down the length of the ship. There was an emergency docking hatch near the back. It wasn't designed to open from the outside, but it had ship-to-ship hookups and, he hoped, a way to activate the door mechanism. Looking back, he could see the bots closing in, surrounding his vessel. They weren't designed to operate in the sort of space he was in now, but Omega was confident that they'd find a way to get to him regardless.

The hatch was above him now, and Omega examined it. There were indeed input and output jacks, but he had no idea if he could connect his wristlink with them. He heard a crash near him, and when he looked, he could see one of the bots coming apart in chunks. He froze, stunned. Something was tearing it to pieces. Omega had a hard time seeing past the debris at this angle, but caught two massive legs in an armoured flight suit striding around his ship, moving to the next closest bot.

That wasn't Swarm reinforcements. Had one of Kazar-Ky's own warlords tracked him down? He prodded his wristlink once more, trying to raise some kind of signal from the hatch. Truthfully, he didn't really care who it was as long as he could make it inside his ship. He could hear confused warbles, and then a crash as the warrior hoisted a bot fully off the ground before smashing it back down.

The other bots had finally taken notice and moved to intercept the attacker. This seemed not to bother the stranger at all. Omega heard the laser blasts of both bots cut short by the screeching grate of metal shorn apart.

He lay still in the silence that followed. His wristlink had proven useless, but at least the bots were gone. Maybe, if he was very careful, he could slip back out to the brush. Perhaps this interloper would assume he'd gone, maybe even distract any other bot patrols if they arrived. Omega was looking for the closest treeline when he felt a great hand close around his ankle. Incredible strength hauled him from beneath the transport, and he yelped as he was hoisted, upside down, into daylight.

He dangled there, disoriented, eyes adjusting, when he heard the newcomer grumble, "Oh. Of course it would be you," before dropping him in a heap. Omega rolled over and looked up. Nothing could have surprised him more.

"Hoonra??"

It was Hoonra. The Karackian stared down, and though Omega had always struggled to read her reptilian expressions, he felt now as if he was a bug she wanted to grind beneath her tridactyl feet. She wore a different jumpsuit than when he'd last seen her, her current attire a mismatch of patchworked interfaces not unlike his own. She returned the sword to the sheath on her back, and Omega could see that it wasn't the ceremonial weapon he'd known her to carry, but a broad piece of sharpened ship's hull. She seemed leaner somehow, harder, but strong as well. She stood, regarding him for just a minute. Then she turned on her heel and stalked off.

"Hoonra? Hoonra, wait!"

Omega was up and after her, and then down again, the pain in his calf flaring. He shouted, but if Hoonra heard, she gave no sign. Steadying himself, he watched her disappear into the trees. He snatched up Kazar-Ky, using the weapon as a walking aid, and hurried after her. She left hardly any trail, but Omega could hear her firing up her ship's preflight systems and followed the sound. The engines started to burn just as he broke through the treeline. He stopped there, and his mouth fell open in shock.

The *Buccaneer II* stood before him, engines primed. The strength went out of him, and Omega collapsed to his knees. The moment stretched as he stared, lost in a vision of a life he barely remembered. He came back to himself as the engines went dark again.

"Hoonra? Hoonra, I...I'm sorry!" The words felt feeble even as he spoke them. He limped forward until his hand rested on the bottom of the entrance ramp, the keypad before him. He looked at it, dry-mouthed. Finally, he stepped back.

"I'll wait," he called, "till you're ready. I'll just...I'll wait out here till you decide." He sat back down in plain view of the cockpit. When there still hadn't been a response by evening light, he prepared himself for a cold night.

At some point before dawn, Omega was awakened by light shining from the *Buccaneer's* open hatch. He sat up, hesitating, before gathering himself and hobbling inside. The ramp, its sounds and textures, were so familiar to him, but he stopped himself as he reached out to touch its sides. This wasn't his ship. Not anymore. Not for as long as he'd acted as the Avatar, and certainly not during his haphazard trek across the Dreamer's Realm. The *Buccaneer* had belonged to a different man, and now to someone else entirely, and Omega found he had to force himself up those last few steps into the main cargo hold.

Hoonra was there, seated by the door that led further into the vessel. Omega felt as though every emotion, every thought that had occurred to him in the last few months crowded into his throat. He opened his mouth to speak, but when nothing came out he coughed, his hand covering his lips. Suddenly, the light stung his eyes.

"I told myself to take off, to forget I saw you here," Hoonra began, after letting him stew a little, "I think I might have said it to myself a hundred times before I had even made it back onboard."

"I'm glad you didn't."

"Why?"

Omega gathered himself. He'd been looking for her for weeks, had rehearsed this precise moment in his head over and over, and now everything he'd hoped to say felt like smoke he was trying to hold in his hand. He began anyway.

"I owe you an apolo—"

"You owe me considerably more than that, Omega Brown. Try again." She stood as she spoke, producing a first-aid kit, moving to inspect Omega's leg without asking.

"You're right, of course." He winced as she sloshed disinfectant across the wound, "Hoonra, what you must have felt when you—"

"Does it feel like this is going well for you?" She pulled a suturing machine from the kit, and Omega forced himself not to yelp. He didn't answer till she'd finished stitching and bound the area.

"No." His leg felt secured, but the treatment had almost been worse than the wound. "No, I barely know what to say. I need to tell you—"

"Yes," she leaned back a little, nodding as though he'd confirmed some assumption for her, "yes, I imagine you feel like you do need to say something. Like the hole in your leg, your needs are often beyond your ability to deal with. The need to apologize. The need to put yourself back in charge. The real question, though, is *why do I need to hear it?*"

Omega said nothing. There was nothing he could say. Eventually he closed his mouth, eyes wandering to the floor.

"Good. Maybe you have learned something after all. I made a mistake when I met you, Omega. I have always been strong. Always successful. I could not conceive of a path I might take in which my sense of honour could fail me. When we first met, I decided to let you own my strength, my abilities, because I thought that leaving my home was the next step in my own journey. I thought to treat you as a stepping stone to my own greater path. Instead, in my naivety, I tied myself to a scoundrel because I thought I would remain unscathed. You were never dishonest about what you really were, I just chose not to see it. You were an honest fool, and I let you make a fool out of me too. Fooled into thinking your money represented loyalty. Fooled into thinking it represented a friend. Look at me, Omega." When he did, she held him there until he felt like squirming.

"You killed us, Omega. You turned your back on us, and we did not survive it." He felt sick. Omega had broken many bones in his life, suffered injuries that had nearly killed him, yet none of them hurt like this. "I mean every word of it, but our lives are no longer so simple. I am afraid we are not finished yet." She held up her scarred hand, the mark which mirrored his own.

"I can feel her. Always. Like a flare in the distance. I imagine your connection with the sword you carry is quite similar. We are bound to them, Omega. We are a part of what they do now."

This was something a little more within his range. "I know. When I finally saw what I'd become, I stole Kazar-Ky away. Without it, his people can't enact his will, but they're hunting me. I ran until I saw what was happening to the folks here, how they live now. I tried to help. I thought maybe I could use Kazar-Ky's power to help free them, or at least protect them, but it's no good. I can't reverse what's been done."

"The sword is called a Ruinblade for a reason. It can accomplish only one thing. Give it to me."

"What?"

"I know where Lyra is. Give me the blade, and I will finish this."

"Hoonra, are you sure it's a good idea to—"

"We are well past the point where you give me orders, Omega. I owe nothing to your inclinations. You have proven yourself weak, without mettle. Give me the sword, and I will finish what you cannot."

Omega wanted to protest but the words wouldn't come. She was right. He'd betrayed her, failed to rescue her. He hadn't even been the one to find her. She had done it all. In the end, taking the scabbard off was easier than he thought it would be.

There was silence when she grasped it, and he thought that Kazar-Ky might say nothing. Then all Omega could hear was the old-god's scream in his mind. The cat's-eye crossguard bulged open, glaring at Hoonra. She crumpled, her body contorting, the mark on her hand tearing open. It took all of Omega's strength to rip the thing from her grip. For a moment he thought she might be dead before she let out a long, shaking breath.

"That hurt tremendously."

"Hoonra," he dropped the blade and ran to hold her, "I'm sorry, I didn't know. I thought, well, I didn't think, but I had no—"

"Enough, enough." She sat up, pushing him away. "You have hurt me again, Omega, through ineptitude." Carefully, she flexed her wounded arm, watching as blood oozed from her scar. "And so we are stuck. I cannot bear the blade, and you cannot be trusted to finish this task. You do not even know what your weapon can do."

"Hoonra, please. Is there nothing I can do to at least make you consider trusting me?"

The Karackian thought for a long time before answering. "There is one thing. The hunt, Omega. The one I completed when we first met. To face an apex predator and best it. That's not something the Omega I knew would have done. The hunt has meaning because it is more than simply slaughtering an animal, and has nothing to do with profit. It is a measure of strength. Of ability. My Elders would have let the Karnax kill me had I not been ready. If I could not live up to a higher standard, I had no place within their hierarchy."

Omega nodded, considering her request. "The people here are defenseless. The Dream has ensnared them all. There are many predators here who prey on them, but there is one creature I found…it will consume every living thing in this city, Hoonra. They have no way to stop it."

"You would hunt this creature, and slay it alone, to prove your worth? With only your sword and your own strength as your weapons?"

"Yes. You'll see my mettle, Hoonra, or you'll see me eaten."

"With the bots here destroyed, it is only a matter of time before The Swarm sends more. Sooner likely, rather than later. Not longer than a day or so at the most. Your hunt will have to start before they arrive. At first light. Tomorrow."

"Fine."

"So be it. Sleep here, in the cargo hold, tonight."

"Thanks."

"It is not a kindness. Locking you in here is the only assurance I have of being able to find you in the morning." Hoonra stood. "I imagine you remember where the light switch is." She left, and he could hear the door lock clicking into place behind her.

The hold was mostly barren except for empty storage containers. Omega propped himself against one of these. He was asleep almost immediately.

Ω

When Omega awoke, the first thing he noticed was that he had slumped over onto his side, and something was jabbing his back. The second thing was the smell of cooked food. He turned over. Hoonra stood there, prodding him with her foot, a plate of something savoury and hot in her hands.

"Are you hungry?"

He took the plate and fork and began shoveling. He had the meal half finished before he realized he still hadn't said anything.

"Sorry," he said, wiping his mouth on his shirt sleeve, "I'm not used to eating around other folks much anymore."

"No, nor to regular meals I would imagine, based on how quickly you inhaled those eggs. You look rough, Omega."

"Well," he confessed around another mouthful of breakfast, "I've been rough." He had expected that admission to hurt, but his mouth was full, and he found he didn't really care. As he ate, Hoonra checked and redressed his leg, saying nothing.

"Thank you. Any sign of the Swarm?"

"Nothing yet, but it will not be long now. Evening, I think, at the latest. They will come in force this time too. Our business must be concluded before then. When you are finished, and properly awake, we will go."

That time came sooner than Omega would have liked. After he'd tested his leg, and Hoonra gave him permission to use the *Buccaneer's* facilities instead of the bushes outside, he returned to the hold and keyed the ramp to open. It wouldn't.

"I told you that I was locking you in." Hoonra moved in front of him, keying the pad so that he couldn't see the code. When the door opened, she motioned for him to go first.

The walk to the beast's lair wasn't too far, but Omega had never been around Hoonra for so long without saying anything. The tension was excruciating. Finally, against his better judgment, he found himself asking, "How did you escape?" From the corner of his eye, he thought he saw her flinch. For a few minutes she didn't say anything.

"She kept me in a dream of our journeys. Pulled memories from me and wove them into something new, but just a bit too familiar. It was like a story that never seemed to end. Eventually, no matter how real it felt, it just did not make sense any longer. I started to fight, started to remember things that did not fit. Eventually she just let me awaken," Hoonra seemed to bite the words as she said them. "I couldn't even goad her into a fight. When I finally woke up, I was weak, partially from lack of proper food, and partially from the energy she took from me. She's vampiric. Draining. My shame upon realizing what had happened..." Hoonra went silent again. Eventually Omega stopped and waited.

"At first I wanted death. For her. For myself. I wanted my strength so I could bring it all down around my head. She knew, of course. She knew, and she laughed. Lyra had used me to regenerate, to grow beyond even what she was ages ago. I do not know how to describe it, except to say that she is more complete now than she ever was. She does not have to split her worship any longer, you see? There is no one to compete with for the veneration and power her worshippers bring. If her abilities could inspire religious obedience when we first met her, now she can create actual truths, delusions so tangible they are really real." She seemed to want to say more, but the words eluded her. Instead, she said, "Lyra would not even let her bots dispose of me. She had become so confident in herself. I tried to assault them. Break them. I could not even dent their plating. She said, when I was ready, when I knew I really wanted it, she would welcome me back. After that, the bots ignored me, as did she. So I ran, then started to travel, gathering my strength. I hunted her patrols and supply lines since I could not hurt her. It was not much, but I could not think of anything else to do. This is how I ended up finding you here."

"But, the *Buccaneer*, how did you find her again?"

“It was in the hold of her temple ship. I do not know if she had saved it, or salvaged it, or recreated it herself from memory, but she had no problem with my taking it. I know it could be her creation, but she feels me, just as I sense her. With or without it, there is nowhere I can go where she won’t know.”

“Does she know you’ve touched the sword?”

“Maybe. One problem at a time, Omega.”

Soon, he had led them to the clearing the beast made. There was no need to convince Hoonra he was telling her the truth. They could see the creature sunning itself, belly huge and round, all six legs akimbo as it snored.

“Well, at least we couldn’t ask for a more willing target.” Omega unholstered his side arm, but Hoonra stopped him.

“This is your honourable fight? Killing a sleeping enemy?”

“Look at it. It obviously gorged itself. We need to stop it now.”

“We are not stopping anything. This is your trial.”

Omega hung his head and took a deep breath. “Right. You’re right.” He re-holstered his sidearm, drawing Kazar-Ky as he stepped out from the bush. “Wake up, ugly.”

The beast snorted and rolled to its feet with a speed Omega did not expect. It looked about itself, dazed, before its dark, angry eyes settled on him. Omega could feel the rumble of its breath in his limbs, and the smell of it promised devastation.

“My,” Omega could hear Hoonra chuckling, “he is a big boy. Good luck, Omega.”

The beast charged, the rhythm of its feet nearly unbalancing him. He steadied himself but the monster was already almost atop him. Omega drew on the power of his sword, Kazar-Ky cackling through his mind. He leaped aside as the beast passed, readying himself for the next charge. The creature obliged him, bellowing in frustration. This time, it kept its head up, its pace slower. It measured him as it approached, swatting tentatively once it was in range. Omega angled Kazar-Ky's point into the paw, his strength and speed bolstered by the old-god, and the beast yowled, backing off. It was angry, but Omega could see it wasn't favouring its paw with any seriousness.

He pressed in, lunging forward as the creature reared back. He swiped at the monster's stomach and haunches, diving into a roll as the thing came crashing down again. When he looked, he could see thin red lines where he'd cut its back sets of legs. The beast was tough. He'd barely drawn blood.

Sensing his hesitation, the creature squared up, backing him towards the entrance of its lair. Omega could feel the cool damp of the cave behind him. There was no way he would let himself be pushed in there. Kazar-Ky cried out in triumph as Omega further opened himself to the blade, taking as much of the old-god's power as he dared. The seething vitriol that was Kazar-Ky flooded his mind, his own consciousness fighting to remain in control. He pushed the blade's anger towards the beast, the mark on his hand flaring with pain.

The monster barrelled in, and its bray was matched in Omega's head by Kazar-Ky's answering howl. The blade began to steam, turning red, then white hot. Omega could feel the weapon's energy coursing through him. He steadied himself and the beast's charge seemed to slow.

Omega ran to meet it. As the creature reached out a paw to smash him, he sprang, landing dexterously on its elbow, running up its shoulder and down its back, dragging Kazar-Ky across its face and neck as he went. At its tail, he jumped again, somersaulting. He landed facing the monster as it reared before the cave, burnt, bloodied, and wailing. As it came down, Omega strode towards it, gripping Kazar-Ky in both hands. It howled defiance, but one last, heavy swing put it down.

As soon as it was done, Omega's knees buckled. Kazar-Ky was still hungry, the old-god pushing against his will. The pain in his scar was nearly unbearable, but he fought, clinging to it, forcing the angry taunts the old-god spewed at him back down. It took longer than usual. It had been some time since he'd last given old Kazar that much leash. Once the pain in his scar returned to a dull, familiar ache, he stood once more.

Hoonra approached from the brush. "An impressive display, certainly, but it will not do. You broke your honour. I said that you must use your own strength, Omega, not that demon of yours."

"Yeah, I hear that Hoonra, but this is my strength now. This is what I've become. For better or worse—and I should clarify that I absolutely assume worse—Kazar-Ky is bound to me, and I to him." He motioned to her hand, "but you know that don't you? You said yourself that there's a similar bond between you and the Dreamer. I'm not proud of what I've become, Hoonra, but if I am a fool, at least I'm not fool enough to lie about it. I understand if you want nothing to do with me."

Omega turned to the carcass behind him. He considered it for a moment before drawing the sword again and proceeding to saw through its hide and hair.

"What are you doing?"

"This thing was going to terrorize the people left here, but now that it's dead, it could just as well feed them. The beings here don't have your strength or your connection to the Dreamer. They're trapped in the Dream, Hoonra, and they can barely look after themselves. If I butcher this and cook it, I can leave some of it for them before it goes bad."

"No, the Swarm will arrive first. You do not have time."

He stopped, wiping his brow. "I did this to them. I can't fix what happened here, but I'm not going to leave them destitute twice. I know you're not staying. I'm sorry I couldn't live up to you, Hoonra. I'm sorry that our time together has been mostly me letting you down. If you can, wherever you decide to go, I hope you'll be well."

Omega bent back to his work. The creature's skin was very tough, and he had to force his body into each swipe. He nearly jumped when her hand touched his shoulder.

"Come," she said.

Ω

The avian child wandered to the ruin's edge as if he were pulled there, a few steps forward, a stumble or two back. Whatever fantasy he lived in, the smell of fresh fruit and cooked vegetables was stronger. As Hoonra and Omega watched from cover, the boy gave a soft hoot of surprise before scarfing down one of the bigger chunks on the platter.

He lifted the prepared meal, considering the small pile of supplies and rations beneath it, before making his dawdling way back into the city.

"That was decent of you. Are you sure you'll have enough supplies yourself?" Omega asked.

"I am very well stocked. It would take you days to butcher a creature of that size with normal equipment, let alone the sword, and the meat would spoil before you could do anything with it. Or, more likely, the Swarm would pulverize you first. Besides, you seemed to think helping them was important."

"It is. And it will be until the Swarm does finally 'pulverize me', as you say." He turned to her. "Speaking of which, you'd better go. They're going to be here soon. Good luck out there, Hoonra." Faking a confidence he certainly did not feel, he extended a hand.

The Karackian measured him before accepting. "The *Buccaneer* is clunky with just one pilot. Too hard to keep bots off my back. My luck might be better if I had a bodyguard."

"Yeah? It just might." Omega felt something he didn't recognize at first, because it had been so long since he'd last felt it. Hope, sprouting like a seed from winter soil, unfurled within him. He chose his next words carefully. "If we do this, we'll have to confront her, Hoonra. This thing we've started has to end, and that only happens with Lyra and the sword destroyed."

She nodded. "I know it. Let us talk more about that." When she turned to go in the direction of the ship, Omega followed.

Episode 7:
The Galaxy's End

The Dreamer's scream raked across the Dreamweave, and none who lived inside it could ignore that sound. It was a scream of defeat, of frustration, and no small amount of fear. As it faded, they began to wake. The Sleeping Crisis was over.

That was eight weeks ago. Now, Inquirer Hillard pressed himself back into the bulkhead as firmly as possible, fighting to keep his recent lunch inside instead of out. Across the cargo space from him, the guards seemed not to notice as they were bumped and jostled just as badly as he was. The Syndicate had not seen fit to provide a proper transport, since the cargo hauler had already been dispatched. The guards were used to this kind of treatment. This sort of landing was, apparently, acceptable.

Hillard closed his eyes, but when that made things worse, he tried looking out the small viewer instead. The landscape beneath him was similar to the other places he'd been. War-torn, rubble strewn about, people rebuilding what they could, leaving what they couldn't. This place was, he was told, better off than many. These people had lived on the edge of the Dreamweave, their society collapsing but without fully crashing to pieces. Other planets—places like Cirella for example—had become uninhabitable for the foreseeable future.

The cargo hauler began its final descent and Hillard gathered himself for what lay ahead. The position of Inquirer was a new one, created by The Syndicate Corporations to help investigate exactly what had happened during the Crisis. In actuality, it felt more and more like Hillard had been given an impossible job just so The Syndicate would have someone to pin the Crisis on. He was used to living a life of luxury as a middling civil politician on a cosmopolitan planet, not traipsing about on backwater worlds, chasing down leads that turned out, again and again, to be someone's misremembered hallucination.

Hillard disembarked, his mercenary guards close behind. The town—generous as descriptions go—was not far away The main street, when he found it, was sodden and mucky, and he stuck to the edges as he made his way onwards. The message he followed came from a colleague who had invited him to meet at a tavern. Hillard had scoffed when he wasn't given a business name. Now, he could see there was only one such place. It seemed to be two stories, maybe a house or some small abode on the top floor. The bottom was open on two sides, awnings stretching out to provide extra space to drink.

There was no door, though there were two mercenary guards similar to his own near the front awning. Hillard scanned the interior as he approached. Only a few barflies, but he could see the other Inquirer he'd come to meet right away. Hillard motioned for the mercenaries to stay by the entrance with the others as he went in. He approached the creature's table and cleared his throat.

"Inquirer Dess?"

The form before him sat forward in its chair, a roughly humanoid suit, full of briny liquid, with a foggy glass bulb for a head. Inside, a cluster of eyeballs on stocks pressed themselves against the glass. Hillard found himself feeling queasy again. The creature reached a pudgy hand up to its helmet, and Hillard worried that it meant to spill itself across the floor. Instead, it flicked a switch and a small voice box lit up.

"Yes." The voice was grainy, flat sounding, "Sit." Dess adjusted a knob on the control plate on his chest, bubbles rising to the top of his tank. He sat back. "I'm sorry to have you meet me in such a remote place, but I wasn't heading back to the central systems just yet."

"It's fine," Hillard glanced about, sighing. "Everywhere I go looks like this, these days."

"Yes. How has your Inquiry been going?"

"Terribly. If it's possible, I might even know less than when the whole thing started.

"My experience has been similar."

"Well, have you found out anything else?" Hillard hissed a little without meaning to. "Anything credible? The only other thing I've heard is about the involvement of some local cults, but even that much is unclear. I have no idea what I'm going to return with at this rate."

Dess's eye stalks retreated into the murk for just a moment, as if assessing something, then reappeared.

"Well, it's possible I do. I found the wreckage of a space station quite by accident, out past one of the asteroid fields at the edge of this sector. There had been a battle, debris everywhere. Still, I managed to find an emergency recording from the central computer core. It had several hours of intact footage from across the station leading up to the end, which I've reviewed. Before I show you, there's a name I've heard, a few times now, connected with all this. Omega Brown."

"I've heard that one too. Sounded a little silly, like an alias. I didn't follow it up."

"I did." Dess held up one exclamatory finger before producing a holodisplay from his suit. The picture of a human male's face, accompanied by an information feed appeared. "He is, apparently, real. The Syndicate had a file on him from a job he was hired for before the Crisis. He was seen in a number of important locations after it started. One source even suggested he was a key player."

"I suppose I heard something similar, but the stories I was told were fanciful at best. Supernatural abilities. Casting lightning, jumping out of flying spaceships. Like I said, I didn't put any stock in it."

"He's in the holo."

"Really?"

Dess's eye stalks bobbed down and then up again inside his helmet, his version of a nod. He brought a video feed up on his display. "Watch."

Ω

The bot stepped over the body of the incapacitated soldier to check on the proximity alarm. There was an escape pod on the scanners. It was moving fast, spinning erratically in its trajectory, and looked like it was going to collide with the installation. Its hatchway was open, and no life forms were aboard. There was no parent ship in sight.

This did not meet the parameters set by the Swarm's Overmind, or by the Mistress. Her attack on the deep-space installation had been fast, the crew succumbing to the Mistress's Dreamweave too quickly to call for help. Even the shifters—Entropic creatures naturally resistant to his Mistress' power—had scattered before their small invading force. This escape pod exceeded expected parameters. It was safest to destroy it.

The bot engaged the targeting system, the computer tracing a bead on the pod and disintegrating it. Parameters normal.

The bot turned to continue its patrol, but another alarm sounded. This one indicated that the pod had managed to call an airlock dock to open for its arrival before it was destroyed. The bot shut the open dock, but the airlock began cycling anyway. Manual inspection was required.

The dock was on the same level, and only one sector away. When the bot arrived, the inner door was open. The bot entered, inspecting the outer airlock for malfunction. It didn't notice Omega Brown stealing around the corner of the corridor to activate the airlock cycle, Hoonra close behind.

The door slid shut. There was a moment of confused warbling from the bot within before the outer door opened, spitting it out into space. Omega leaned back against the wall.

"That was slick. Where the hell is everyone?"

"I told you." Hoonra walked across the hall to stand before a slumped over sentry. "Lyra has become immensely powerful. This one is not dead, just sleeping. The Dreamweave empowers her even as she creates it. Our connection to this problem makes us unique; no one else near her can remain unaffected save for the bots, and possibly the shifters. I am not even sure if *we* will remain lucid."

"Still think we can call the *Buccaneer* in when we need it?"

"The controls are all set, but I think you would say that we will need to keep our fingers crossed."

Omega nodded. "Right, so just about as certain as we ever are. Let's go."

The duo jogged farther down the corridor until they came to a control hub. The installation was Kazar-Ky's, his battle station for summoning the banished Lords of Entropy back to this universe. Omega was already familiar with the controls. He scanned the station.

"Lyra's almost reached the bridge. It looks like the operators here managed to set up some blocks before they lost consciousness, but they won't last." Omega showed Hoonra a floor schematic. "The controls for the portal mechanism are here, but Lyra and her entourage have only made it this far. I wonder if—"

"Yes," Hoonra answered as if she could see his thoughts, "she can sense us. She'll feel the Ruinblade's presence this close, and she'll certainly feel me."

Omega widened his scans, then brought up a new schematic, this one showing a whole wing of the station. "You're right. Scanners show small pods of bots deployed at choke points on her trail. We can't approach her without meeting them." A light started flashing. "Her ship, her gigantic temple thing, it's sending shuttles." Omega frowned as he watched the readout. "A lot of shuttles. Supplies?"

"No. She wants us. She wants the Ruinblade."

"This was a trap?"

"Probably," Hoonra considered this for a moment. "If it was though, what does that change?"

"Nothing." Lyra needed to be stopped, and confronting her without the Ruinblade would only leave Omega vulnerable to her power. Only Hoonra's connection with Lyra, combined with the power of Kazar-Ky trapped within the sword, would help them against her.

As Omega watched, the first of the shuttles flew past Kazar-Ky's now deactivated Dreadnought, and began its final approach. It would begin disgorging fresh bots in a few minutes. "Okay. They haven't been able to activate any of the internal station defenses yet, so as long as we can keep the pressure on, we should have a chance."

"Omega."

When he looked up from the display, he froze. Hoonra stood totally still, facing a mob of shifters who had gathered silently behind them. Hoonra reached slowly towards her sword. Omega stopped her.

"Hang on," he stepped forward. "You all remember me, don't you. You know what I carry." With a flourish, Omega drew the Ruinblade from his back. Kazar-Ky's bright orange cat's eye opened from the crossguard. It blinked, sluggish, and Omega felt none of the usual malice that drawing the weapon normally brought on. Even Kazar-Ky was feeling the effects of the Dreamweave. Omega hoped the shifters wouldn't notice.

With the blade drawn before them, the shifters began falling about themselves. Some seemed to want to take it from him, shuffling forward before falling back. Others fell to a knee, their arms upraised.

"Where is Kitt?" Omega called them to silence. "Where is the shifter who knew me?" From midway through the crowd, one approached. As it moved, it changed, its body reshaping itself into a semblance of the woman Omega remembered.

"Hello Omega." Her voice was as silken as always. "Have you come to take your mantle as Avatar back?"

"You know I haven't. It's over. Lyra has nearly won." Without warning Kitt howled, an aching, defeated sound, and the other shifters joined in.

"She cannot," Kitt moaned, holding her head, "she cannot win, she cannot. You were supposed to stop her. You were supposed to lead us." She seemed incoherent, lost.

"You want victory?" Omega stepped forward. "You want her stopped? You want revenge for my betrayal? Take it. Get to the dreadnought. Lyra is focused on us now, she won't suspect you any longer. Use Kazar-Ky's vessel and destroy this place while you still can. Do this, in the name of the Avatar you once followed."

Kitt looked up, straightening. The other shifters were affected as well, the authority in Omega's voice calling them back.

"He is the Lord of Betrayal, Kitt. Destruction is his nature. Follow him."

The shifters turned to each other. Something passed between them, some message they understood. Kitt looked back for a moment, and Omega realized that she was looking at the sword. Then, as a mass, they turned and disappeared into the station.

Ω

"What you just saw happened roughly two standard hours before the station's destruction."

Hillard sat back, confused. "Those things he met, they listened to him; he is more important than I thought. What's a Ruinblade?"

Dess shrugged. "The sword he carries, I believe. And it seems that your rumour about cults might hold more weight than you realized. In any case, this Omega is skilled and well-armed, and he has allies. You should see what that sword of his can do." Dess fast-forwarded the feed for a moment and then hit play again.

Ω

The corridors here were much wider and taller and, this close to the central command area, had been afforded some actual view plates of the space around the station. Hoonra stepped up to the closest of these.

"Omega," she pointed.

Omega could see laser fire flashing, and it took him a moment to realize that Lyra's vessel had begun firing on the dreadnought. Kazar-Ky's ship, in turn, had opened fire on the station itself.

"The shifters listened."

"They have diverted her for now, but it won't last. We don't have much time."

As if cued, the sound of bot speech warbled up to meet them. A few hundred feet down the hall, a patrol was approaching, ten or twelve strong.

"We should not have waited. There is no cover here."

169

"We'll be fine." Omega drew the Ruinblade from his back. "They want us to run to her. I'm getting pretty tired of being herded along."

He concentrated on his scar, his lifeline with Kazar-Ky, and the old god's vitriolic consciousness welled up within him.

Omega began to jog towards the bots, and as he entered a better range, they opened fire. He used Kazar-Ky's power, enhancing his speed and strength. Their shots fell wide, and as Omega closed in, the Ruinblade began to glow white-hot.

Omega was upon them in a moment, the sword shearing through their frames, their clustered formation within the hallway making the job that much easier. The blade hissed and spat as he walked back through the wreckage.

Kazar-Ky's voice whispered within Omega, congratulating him for using the sword's power, urging him to lose himself in that flow. The words were poison, as always, but Omega found that they fit his mood. He was of a mind for ending things.

"If I never see another bot, it will still have been about a hundred too many. Let's get to the bridge and finish this."

They carried on to the annex, dispatching two more bots that appeared as they went. A series of explosions sounded, distant, foreboding. The double doors to the station's central control room lay open. Apparently, Lyra had decided they'd been stalled enough.

The room inside was big, though not as cavernous as Lyra's own Temple-Ship. Three stories of catwalks and stairways connected various control hubs. At the central apex, a large platform had been erected to house the controls for the portal. There were three or four bots about too, working at the controls, but they ignored Hoonra and Omega entirely. The duo looked at each other, then Hoonra started to climb. Omega followed.

Lyra awaited them. Omega had not seen her since before Kazar-Ky had taken him, months ago, on Cirella. That last time, she'd been unable to live without the aid of an incubator, her projection into his thoughts that of a demanding little girl with mismatched eyes. The woman standing before him bore those same eyes, but was otherwise totally changed. She wore an elegant robe instead of the gown he'd seen before. She was beautiful, sleek and strong, her vitality an almost metaphysical presence he could sense. Despite this, Omega found that she reminded him of a parasite, full and engorged.

"Hello, Omega." Her voice was soft, warmly seductive, with just a hint of its old petulance.

"Dreamer. Giving up after all that?"

Lyra smiled and turned away from them. "Oh, no. I'm sure you saw the shuttles. Kazar-Ky's servants have managed to resist me where his soldiers could not, but they're hardly winning. My ship has almost disabled them, and my reinforcements will be here shortly, not that they're needed. The truth is I was waiting for her." The Dreamer smiled warmly at Hoonra.

"For what reason?" Hoonra crossed her arms, and Lyra looked genuinely confused at this.

"Why, to offer a chance to rejoin me, or course. You were so angry when you left, Hoonra dear, and it's true, I've carried on without you. Still, you are my Avatar, *my* Chosen, and there is even more we could accomplish together. Look at him," Lyra pointed to Omega without regarding him, "look what my Sibling has done for him. He destroyed that patrol down the hallway without hesitation, didn't he? Kazar-Ky's strength is his to wield, and look how it's empowered him. You didn't just leave, Hoonra; I let you go so you could see it for yourself."

Omega opened his mouth, but the look on Hoonra's face stopped him. She was listening, actually listening. In the same way Kazar-Ky had a lifeline straight to Omega's thoughts, Lyra could do the same to Hoonra.

"But there's more." Lyra stepped closer, her eyes intense, feverish. "Kazar-Ky's power lies only in destruction, in betrayal, but mine rests in dreams. In inspiration. Creation. This can be your power too, my Avatar." She lowered her voice now, her words confessional. "We've never been properly connected, you and I, Hoonra. You are strong, stubborn in a way I didn't understand. I always had to trick you, use you, to gain power from our connection. No more. You know now what my power could become. Look how it has reshaped me. If you will come to me willingly, if you will simply use the power I share with you, think of all we could create together."

Kazar-Ky had been quiet up to this point, but his voice came screaming back. It was fear Omega heard, anger and desperation. The Ruinblade demanded he run Hoonra through, now before she could respond. Omega fought that voice back down. Lyra turned to him with a knowing smile.

"He wants you to act, doesn't he, Omega? My Sibling wants you to attack Hoonra, right now."

"Omega?" Hoonra spoke slowly, as if struggling to understand.

"It doesn't matter what the sword wants. I'm in control, not him."

"Yet you still carry him, still brought him here with you. Too dangerous to leave it behind. But what if I were to wrest it from you, use it to complete the station as Kazar-Ky intended? Dangerous of you to risk it. Why not put it in an escape pod and fire it into a black hole?" Lyra pinned him with her eyes. "It is because you don't want to leave it alone, do you? No matter what you say, you like what it does for you. The power. And it's only a matter of time." She turned back to Hoonra, speaking as if Omega had disappeared. "The voice never stops, not fully. How long can he resist it, Hoonra? How long until the blade finally breaks through. Ten years? Twenty? And when it does, Omega will go right back to being everything he was when he abandoned you."

Lyra moved between them, and Omega would have struck her had he not seen Hoonra let Lyra place a hand on her bicep. "We can end this now, Hoonra. We can make this right, today." Standing beside Hoonra, Lyra now regarded Omega with open disdain. "Kill him, end this struggle, and we will create a better version of this universe together."

Omega's mouth went slack, and Hoonra regarded him, calculating, as he'd seen her do before a particularly hard fight. Her words echoed that slow consideration.

"He is a small man, and frail. He is weak in ways I have never approved of. I cannot say that I thoroughly trust him. I also cannot say that I believe you. I have seen what your power creates. Ruined worlds and stupefied refugees. Citizens stranded, emaciated by fantasies they cannot escape while you grow strong and fat on their suffering. You are a leech, Dreamer." Hoonra moved away from Lyra and stood by Omega again. "The galaxy can only improve in your absence."

Lyra's face became drawn, and Omega thought she looked very much like a punished child. She glared at Hoonra for a moment, and the Karackian shifted slightly where she stood, flexing her scarred hand.

"It's over Lyra." Omega didn't want to lose the moment. "There's nothing left but—"

Hoonra's arm swung, catching Omega in the solar plexus, hurling him backwards. He landed in a sprawl, the Ruinblade flying from his grasp. He could hear the Dreamer laughing as he struggled to catch his breath.

"It's an extraordinary skill you learned, Omega, to be able to hold my Sibling at bay through the scar that marks you. Perhaps you might have considered teaching it to Hoonra before bringing her back into my presence." As he struggled to sit up, he watched as Hoonra turned towards him, her eyes clouded over, milky and distant. "I let Hoonra go, Omega. Did you really think I would hesitate to bring her back if I thought she would deny me? It would be easier, of course, if she didn't fight, but one does what one must. Hoonra dear," Lyra leaned towards the Karackian's ear, whispering theatrically, "throw him over the railing and break him, won't you? I need to retrieve my Sibling."

Ω

The image between Hillard and Dess shook a little as another explosion wracked the station, then the feed flicked and turned to static.

174

"What?" Hillard felt irate. "That's it? How do we know if he survived? How do we know if any of them survived? For goodness sake, Dess, this is almost worse than not knowing anything at all."

Dess held up a finger, his eye stalks turning towards the entrance. "There's another reason I asked you to meet me here. What time is it?" Hillard checked and told him. "Good, any minute now."

Hillard scanned the street, and a few moments later, he saw the big alien rounding the corner of the block. Her head and face were partially covered by a hood. She carried no weapon, but her bulk and movements were unmistakable.

Hillard watched as the alien approached the canteen. She didn't look at either of them as she sat at the bar. Once her back was to them, Hillard looked at Dess with alarm. In response, Dess stood, stepping behind her, motioning for Hillard to follow.

"Hoonra." Dess didn't ask, his voice box emitting the word the same way a person might throw a gauntlet.

To her credit, the alien gave no sign of having heard, staring down at the table and waiting for her drink. One or two of Dess's eye stalks looked about nervously, and Hillard felt his nerve begin to slip. "We want Omega," he blurted.

This had the desired effect. Hoonra turned, slowly, and stood. Hillard craned back his neck as Dess pressed his eyes against the top of his bulb.

"I suppose I have been waiting for someone like you."

Dess stepped back in, "We have questions about some recent events you appear to have been involved in."

Hoonra looked between them, considering the entrance again as she did. Dess was just about to motion for the guards when her posture slumped.

"Fine. It's been long enough. I suppose you wish to know what happened to Omega?"

"Some of it we know," Dess replied, and Hillard was impressed with his ability to project confidence. "But I would hear whatever you would tell us about your confrontation with this Dreamer." Dess motioned to the table he and Hillard had occupied. Hoonra shifted herself and took the seat offered.

They joined her, and sat for a moment, watching Hoonra examine her hands. Her bulk seemed curled in on itself, as if awaiting a strike. Dess began, gently.

"We found a holo, a security recording. You and this Omega were in it. You were working together, but then that changed. You struck him, and shortly after the feed cut off. We need to know what happened."

At the mention of striking Omega, Hoonra flinched. She continued to look at her hands, clenching and unclenching them. Hillard could hear her tail swish below the table. Slowly, she began.

"I wasn't in control any longer. You have to understand that. The Dreamer...I did not know she could, but she—she took my mind again. Away from me. I was her instrument. I could see myself acting, I could watch my own body, but I had no...I could not..."

"Couldn't what?" Hoonra looked at Dess, her expression pleading.

"She *made* me break him. I could not stop it. She made me, with my own hands, like some animal," A tremor ran through her. "She made me kill him, and then she gave me back my mind, so I could properly feel what I'd done."

Hillard sat back, letting out a breath he didn't know he was holding. "What happened then?"

"I ran," Hoonra said.

"What?"

It took Hoonra a moment to repeat herself. "I ran. I just—" She slumped again, looking back at her hands which she continued rubbing together. "I was lost. The station was coming apart, and I had...well, after what I had already done to Omega, I ran."

"And Lyra? What happened to her?" Hillard looked as though he'd swallowed a particularly pointy insect.

"Destroyed in the explosion."

"You're sure?" Dess leaned in, his eye stalks all pressed against the glass.

"Nothing could have survived that blast. It was a miracle my ship was not torn apart in the shockwave. I was only lucky to have left when I did."

Hillard and Dess looked at each other, and then back to Hoonra. "Well, eh, Hoonra, that's an incredible story. Really. It's one, I think, that my superiors back in the Syndicate would love to hear." Hillard stood, motioning for the guards by the entrance.

"No. Please. I cannot leave this place. These people need help. You must understand, after everything that has happened, after what I have done, all I want now is to try and help others heal."

"Yes, well," Hillard ignored her, "no one is saying this needs to be a formal arrest. Not your fault, and all that. I'm sure we can get you back here in a flash." He stood, moving back from the table and motioning to the guards. Dess followed his lead.

Hoonra seemed unarmed, while the guards carried rifles, stun batons, and armour. They surrounded her. Hillard began to consider how they would keep her intact for the ride back, or if they ought to incapacitate her now. His attention snapped back when, without warning, Hoonra lifted the closest guard and used him to batter the man behind him. The other two guards pulled their batons, but Hoonra was faster, slapping one of the men so hard he spun on the spot, leaning back to kick the other over as she did it. It was finished in a few seconds. Hillard wasn't sure he'd had time to blink.

Hoonra stepped towards Hillard and Dess, and both Inquirers shrank back. "I am staying," said Hoonra quietly, "and I will thank you for respecting that decision." She walked backwards, keeping an eye on the Inquirers until she'd reached the entrance, then she jogged off down the street. Hillard took a moment to compose himself, while Dess looked out after Hoonra.

"She is gone," Dess said. "I don't have the resources here, now, to mount a search. I'd have to come back. Requisition more men from the Syndicate. We don't have much to work with, but if I show them this recording—"

"You do that." Hillard watched in disgust as one of his guards began to pick himself up. He walked to the entrance. Dess called after him, but Hillard ignored him. He was going to go back to the port, catch the first ride out, and turn in his resignation. The hell with this assignment.

Ω

Hoonra watched from an alley further down the street as Hillard, still shaking his head, walked back to the landing pad at the edge of the village. Behind her, a shadow detached itself from the alley.

"Thanks for that." Omega Brown peered over her shoulder into the street, patting her on the back. "That was actually quite a performance. You think they bought it?"

"One of them, yes."

"Then I guess I owe you another drink."

Hoonra chuckled. "I imagine you'll be able to work the debt off. Being a bodyguard pays well enough. You were right though, they seem far less interested in discovering the truth of the Crisis than they are in finding a way to explain why it is not important."

"As governments go, the Syndicate has never been properly interested in helping people. That's one of the reasons why bribes go such a long way. I've talked to the most important people in town. A few of the citizens might be able to identify us but the community leaders will deny it, at least long enough for us to disappear again. Was the fella with the bulb head there?"

"He was."

179

"Thought so. He might be the only one who's actually paying attention. It'll be good to get him off our trail. Come on."

Omega pulled Hoonra's shoulder, leading her back towards the safehouse he'd found for them. In an hour or two they'd make their way back to the *Buccaneer's* hiding place and take off. "Say, how did you tell them I died?"

"They seemed stretched to the limits of their belief with the little I was honest about," Hoonra shrugged. "I kept it simple, told them I broke you with my hands."

Omega stopped at a panel at the alley's end and gave a particular knock. The panel slid back. "Broke me? You said it like that? I think hanging around with me is starting to rub off on you. You're certainly getting more dramatic." He stepped aside as Hoonra entered.

A murder and the explosion were simple explanations, and, in the end, perhaps the best choice. A curt ending, and a final one. Certainly, it seemed more likely, more possible, than what had actually happened.

Ω

With his immediate connection with the Ruinblade lost, Omega felt the Dreamweave begin to submerge him. He couldn't focus, his eyes locking on to Hoonra only as she grabbed hold of him, dragging him to the edge.

"Hoonra," he kicked feebly, "you have to fight it. The scar, you have to concentrate on—"

She threw him, tossing him sideways the way she might dispose of a bag of rubbish. He rotated as he flew, activating his boots to steady himself unsuccessfully before he smacked into the wall. He skidded as he fell, landing hard on the gangway below.

Omega's head spun, his senses totally muddled. He could feel vibrations, Hoonra's steps closing in. Beneath it, somewhere in the room, Kazar-Ky was protesting. This last thought fled his mind as he felt himself hoisted up. The room gave another hazy rotation and Omega saw he was dangling above Hoonra's head, waiting to be dashed against the ground below.

"The scar," Omega croaked, "the scar is the way. Fight, Hoonra, I know you can." He felt her tense for just a moment, and fired his boots again, shooting out of her grasp to sputter out a few feet farther down the gangway.

The Dreamweave continued to assault his senses, but Omega could see Hoonra clutching her now-singed hand. The damage didn't look like much, but it was the scar she focused on. Hoonra flexed her hand, and then pulled her arm back, crying out. Omega had never seen her do that before. He could hear another voice, Lyra's, shouting in frustration. Hoonra rocked back and forth, keening.

"Yes, Hoonra." Omega tried to drag himself towards her. "You've done it before, you can do it again. Fight her off. Focus on the pain in your scar, feel that connection to her."

Hoonra had become quiet, her hand opening and shutting as she flexed it. Omega could see that her eyes were no longer clouded. She breathed deeply, deliberately, then she stood up. Immediately, Omega felt the influence of the Dreamweave dissipate. She stepped towards him, looking down.

"She is very powerful, but I am learning too. Come." Omega took her extended hand, following her back up the scaffold. At the top, Lyra looked decidedly like a brat caught in the act of doing something she should not. Hoonra swayed a little before her, then stood firm.

"You will need to do better than that, Dreamer." She flexed her hand once more. Lyra sneered.

"Please. If I were worried, I'd have had the bots shoot you both while you fought. Instead, I needed them to finish."

Behind her, Omega and Hoonra could see two bots maneuvering the sword between them. They lifted the Ruinblade, fitting it into a slot in the terminal. Once the sword was fitted, they turned it like a great key.

"No!"

"Oh, yes," Lyra replied, drawing the word out with a hiss. Behind her, a green light flashed on. The station began drawing on the sword's power, its energy coursing through the metal casing. There was a moment where it seemed nothing would happen. Then, through the window, Omega could see a current of iridescent energy crackling across the massive antenna suspended from the outside of the control room, like a lightning rod flashing against the darkness of space.

"It works." Lyra breathed the words as if she wasn't sure she could believe it. As they watched, the energy collected at the tip of the spire grew bigger, wider, like a pool of water leaking across stone. At first the middle was bright white, but when Omega peered into the widening space, he could see a different star-scape begin to emerge. Gas clouds, and nebulae, all swirling, like fish beneath the surface of a pond. A different and older universe looked back.

"Sisters!" Lyra shrieked, triumphant, her voice echoing not just through the room, but inside his skull as well. Her face had taken on a gaunt quality in that weird light, and Omega thought she looked like some kind of wraith. "Come back to this universe, Sisters, come back and serve me!"

There were no words in response, but after a moment there was a sound, a low vibration, that he could feel in his chest. It grew, a pressure building against the inside of his lungs, his eardrums. Something was getting closer.

The station shifted, the whole structure shaking, just a little, and there was another flash of light. From the right viewport, Omega saw the dreadnought colliding with the space station, driving itself into the structure. As he watched, the ship ploughed through a chunk of the installation, tearing it completely away before both of them finally exploded. Debris flew, and the station took even more damage. A full collapse was inevitable.

Power blinked out for just a moment and then stuttered back, some flailing emergency system working against final destruction. Power to the spire became sporadic, the computers flickering on and off, but the portal remained, the humming sensation growing more powerful. The clouds in the nebula began to roil and reshape, but they were pushing upwards now, bursting towards the surface of the portal. Something had indeed heard Lyra's call. The nebula on the other side breached the plane of the portal, reaching through like some delicate, alien finger, coiling towards the station's bridge.

Omega was shouting, but Hoonra couldn't hear. He tried again. "Call the ship! Hoonra, it's over! Call the ship!"

She did, but when she'd turned back to Omega, he was airborne again, using his boots to fly back up. He landed, grabbing the sword, trying desperately to pull it out of the slot. Lyra shrieked and flew at him, tearing at his hands. Hoonra was sure the station would fall apart around her.

Omega felt as if his bones were rattling. The Ruinblade was stuck fast; the ordeal now inescapable. Worse, Lyra was screaming madly in his ear, shrieking and laughing at once, stopping him from getting any kind of serious hold. It occurred to him that she didn't know any better how this would turn out than he did. The world was ending, and Omega Brown was at its centre.

Before him, the portal had expanded enough to consume part of the antenna, and it kept growing. The sound, the pressure he felt coming from it, was omnipresent now, and Omega thought he could hear distinct voices in it, personalities speaking eager words he could not understand.

"Yes, Sisters," Lyra screamed, triumphant. "Here, I'm here! Bring yourselves to me!"

Pressure, a new pressure, on Omega's shoulders and chest. It forced him up and back, taking him away from Lyra, from the sword. It was Hoonra. With a tremendous heave, she hauled Omega up and away from the command station, even as he shouted at her to leave him.

Then, Hoonra ran.

With all of her strength and conditioning, Hoonra bolted, slinging Omega like a sack of vegetables over one shoulder as she ran to the nearest emergency hatch. She was speaking, but Omega's brain felt split. He could still hear the echoes from across the void, could still hear

Lyra's mad coaxing. Something had changed, though. Lyra wanted the power, but Omega wondered if the other entities actually wanted to share it. He saw Hoonra's mouth moving again.

"What?"

"The ship, you fool! Get in!" A hatchway slid open and Hoonra pushed him inside, dragging him down the extended airlock passage, and dumping him on the other side.

The *Buccaneer*. Omega was sitting by the emergency dock in the cargo hold. He collected himself, following Hoonra to the bridge.

As they detached, Omega could see the portal had consumed the entire antenna and much of the bridge. In his mind, he could still feel the quarrel intensifying. Lyra was demanding something her counterparts were not interested in giving. Omega wondered who would dominate whom. He needn't have bothered. Somewhere inside the station, the power generator finally kicked off. The explosion started in the station's core and spread, tearing everything to pieces. A whole wing detached, spinning into Lyra's temple ship as the vessel tried to move away.

The *Buccaneer* kept just ahead of the blast, Hoonra punching the thrusters to full as the station sent debris in every direction.

There was a scream, a splintering feeling inside Omega's mind, and his eyes were dragged back towards the spire. The power coursing through the sword was finally cut and, as if draining away, the portal was closing, sucking in everything in its vicinity as it went.

Hoonra piloted the *Buccaneer* expertly, dodging the flying chunks of station, and blasting off for clearer space. Behind them, Lyra,

Kazar-Ky, and all of their works fell back into the void they had come from as the portal finally closed. There was a moment then, before the jump to warpspace where Omega realized he felt nothing. No voices. No pressure. No guilt. Just him and Hoonra.

Hoonra initiated the jump, and for the first time in a long while, Omega Brown felt free.

Acknowledgements

My deepest thanks to Donald Webb, and all the readers and editors of *BewilderingStories.com*, for first allowing Omega to put on his rocket boots and fly. Thanks also to Lucas, Roddenberry, Butler, King, LeGuin, Moorecock, Tolkien and many, many others I don't have room to mention here. I have no stories without yours first.

About The Author

Tom Vaine is a high school teacher working in Wellington County, Ontario. He has a Master's Degree focused on avant-garde science fiction, though he has a soft spot for the Golden Age stuff as well. When he isn't reading or writing up weird worlds, Tom like to spend time relaxing with his wife Danielle and daughter Rosie-Jane.